The Universe as Performance Art

Stories

by

Colby Smith

The Universe as Performance Art
by Colby Smith
ISBN: 978-1-913766-15-3

Cover Art by David Rix

Publication Date: 2024

Contents

For Ryan Pitchford and Marcus Pavilonis.

Stars scribble on our eyes the frosty sagas,
The gleaming cantos of unvanquished space…

—Hart Crane, "Cape Hatteras"

ACKNOWLEDGMENTS

The reprinted pieces in this collection all originally appeared in anthologies related to the Neo-Decadent international arts movement: "Somnii Draconis" in *Drowning in Beauty: The Neo-Decadent Anthology* (Snuggly Books, 2018); "Cooking Australia" in *The Neo-Decadent Cookbook* (Eibonvale Press, 2020); "Hellenic Dropout" in *Neo-Decadence Evangelion* (ZAGAVA, 2023).

The Universe as Performance Art

An audience gathered.
They came to witness the creation-at-once-destruction.
Before the audience's nothingness there was Her.
What was Form to Her?
What was Living?
Was Form the child or mother to Living?
How absent to the audience She was.
How present, yet.
Presence commanded all.
Presence seduced the nothingness that remained.
She took the stage alone.
The faint, embryonic light was Hers.
The profuse, hanging shadows were Hers.
For Her sake the shadows and light writhed in concert.
Yet She was never nor will She ever be truly alone.
The first work, the first art.
They came to witness.
No distinction between art and work.
Work, art, art, work—preordained.
Before that stage She had no body.
Before that stage She had no skull.
Before that stage all She had was *will*.

Through Her will, Her brain matter coagulated.
Nerves took root.
Those nerves would never budge again.
The nerves branched out infinitely, indefinitely.
Dendrites//axons.
No cartography possible for those dendrites.
No astronomy possible for those axons.
Through Her will Her body vulcanized.
Un-blood steaming into blood.
Un-flesh frosting into flesh.
Her will produced inelegant motions.
Subsequent motions—elegant.
Gnosis impenetrable.
Agnosis compulsory.
She bore neither beauty nor loathsomeness.
Her hinged jaws creaked as She spoke.
Incipient babble, then words.
She twined the words together into a program.
A program to dictate the first work.
A program to realize the first art.
The words pealed across the residual nothingness.
The audience listened after that first sound.
They were curious, baffled, bored.
By the program's intermission some went deaf again from the peals.
A dagger of condensed hydrogen manifested.
The hilt roasting Her palm.
Ur-white flesh turned mauve by the burns.
Her gaze slithered over the blade.
She signaled to the audience.
A specter from the audience approached Her.
Its nudity shone through the oblivion.
A sculpture of nickel rose from the nothingness.
The nickel swam and gelled into a relief.
That relief showed a cosmos of genitalia.

The specter prostrated itself on it.
She took its testicles in Her hand.
Dense with the weight of Beginning.
She lifted the scrotum.
Delicate with the weight of Ending.
The testicles were unevenly shaped.
The left testicle's oval curvature never interrupted.
The right testicle's curvature had no shape or symmetry.
She took the dagger and slit the scrotum.
The dagger merely abrased the flesh.
She hacked away until ur-blood leapt out of the wound.
Until the scrotum came off in Her hands.
The specter did not scream.
It laughed.
Specter disintegrated.
Relief disintegrated.
Audience only accepted what they witnessed.
A wake without mourning.
A wake so full of primordial black there was no significance to *black* or *wake*.
She dissected the testicles.
The first fruits.
The sperm was hardened into stones.
She extracted the ossified sperm.
Shoved them inside Her in succession.
The stones melted.
She leaked—then poured.
Her stomach swelled-swelled-swelled.
Swollen stomach *split//burst*.
Doused in obsidian afterbirth.
Bird of a million colors.
Bird of a thousand eyes.
Bird of a hundred wings.
Bird of no face—anonymous.
Remaining still, they witnessed.

The bird preened its polar genitals.
Plucked out gobs of black afterbirth from its plumage.
Her tongue and throat contorted at the sight.
Vocals, not words anymore.
The first song.
Newborn bird sublimated upon hearing bass and tenor at once.
Dripping afterbirth hung in midair in time with hideous notes.
Throbbed and shuddered in spatiotemporal orgasm.
Coiled and coagulated into shining matter.
The matter was spherical and compact.
The matter was hot beyond hot beyond hot.
She designated it *stella*.
She plucked a chunk of stella from the progenitor of stella.
She blew on the stella and it scattered across the stage.
The stella hung fungal then bred whorishly.
The stage was shining now.
The audience's viscera hummed viscerally.
They had seen the stella.
Beauty—the impending Destroyer of Creation.
She reached into Her mouth.
Pulled a tooth.
Another, another.
Till nothing but nude gums in Her hinged maw.
She crushed the teeth in Her hands.
Audience winced.
The enamel molded into something akin to Her.
Something like the audience.
The first astronaut.
The astronaut reproduced like the very stella from which it was born.
(*plus time plus time plus*)
Soon a legion.
Later a species.

Pheromone Literature

Five million years of destroying planets cradling civilizations that produced primitive eyesore art passed before the nomadic Konchuu concluded that they had to take the initiative to create art that reflected their conception of the universe's aesthetic zenith.

The Konchuu were a species of comparative aestheticians. They had no artistic tradition to call their own but were constantly preoccupied with cataloging and compartmentalizing art wherever and however it manifested. Their mothership had already propelled them through several galaxies beyond their home planet—a hothouse world characterized by mercury-red vegetation covering every continent—which was rendered uninhabitable by the proliferation of invasive protists that hitchhiked on a small asteroid originating from an adjacent planetary system. They turned the oceans black and released copious amounts of chlorine into the atmosphere. All native life had gone extinct except for the Konchuu.

Remote cortical implants in the Konchuu's three-lobed brains enabled the superficial beauty they found in wayward stars, uninhabited satellites, and passing comets to fuel their mothership. No Konchuu axon or dendrite were idle whenever a celestial body was in the mothership's field of vision.

Konchuu bodies did not degenerate with age or accumulated stress. Their superchitinous exoskeletons were more durable than granite, while the musculature and viscera were as light as plastic.

They did not age past imago-maturity. They were immune to apocalypse within their mothership.

The Konchuu's quest began gestating among them four centuries before the first chlorinating protist arrived from that neighboring planetary system. This collective monomania metamorphosed from a crude, fervent, masturbatory mysticism to the species' *suicidal destiny*. They would have destroyed their homeworld themselves had the chlorine-holocaust not displaced them first.

Yet their suicidal destiny completely clouded over the more utilitarian pursuit of a new planetary settlement. They gauged the existential worthiness of any given planet they encountered based on the art its native species produced. Said planet being destroyed was always a probability of *one*.

The Konchuu's methodology of comparative aesthetics was interventionist. Before destroying a particular planet, they would first conduct experiments on the planet's native civilization: ecological proxy war; genetic coups; consciousness-fissioning; looting continental plates; gelatinizing aquatic bodies; scalping atmospheres. The sole, futile motivation behind such comprehensive transmutation was to coerce these species into producing art that would bring the Konchuu's quest to a close.

They were, symbolically, food for the Konchuu. Whether the food is eaten or decomposes by itself, food must inherently be destroyed to be *food in itself*.

Eventually such food ceased to nourish the Konchuu, and they were paying for their automatic gluttony. Their three-lobed brains were blunted to all beauty and, as their nerves baked into wires, the mothership decelerated parsec by parsec until it stalled altogether around the peripheral of a minor spiral galaxy. There was nothing left to do but fast.

Poetically, it became the burden of the Konchuu to exact the universe's aesthetic zenith themselves or face an apocalypse of atrophy.

The medium was to be literature.

The Konchuu fashioned parallelogrammical slabs from piles of their magenta fecal matter strewn haphazardly around the mothership to serve as the functional skeleton of a Konchuu text. They had no written language and were anatomically devoid of a vocal apparatus. They, instead, communicated interpersonally through pheromone signals. Consequently, the Konchuu smeared the slabs of fecal matter with these pheromones—a chemical cuneiform—to remove any obscurity from what the Konchuu desired to convey.

Every member of the Konchuu species participated in manufacturing pheromone literature which, for the first time since their exodus began, necessitated a radical division of labor. There came the Defecators, who timed defecation with the accuracy of a circadian rhythm to meet the Quota for fecal tablets. There were the Sculptors, who took the fecal matter provided by the Defecators and molded it into slabs of standardized dimensions. There were the Emitters who secreted a continuous haze of pheromones that each bore diagnostic chemical signatures, the frequency of which was preordained by the Quota. The Scribes were responsible for composing the pheromone literature. Then there were the Beholders, who read over the pheromone literature that once more accelerated and sustained the flight of the mothership.

Pheromone literature was an objective art. Every syllable of every sentence was unambiguous and could not be interpreted beyond the original, superficial intended meaning. The concepts pheromone literature interrogated—the scenarios it depicted, the very grammar through which it was all conveyed—were of exclusive understanding to the Konchuu; nor could it ever be adapted or translated even into pheromones emitted by another wayfaring species of aestheticians. Thus, the Konchuu declared pheromone literature incorruptible, the *arch-expression*.

The Konchuu Renaissance finally began. From dormant collective memories of their homeworld—the taxonomy of the native organisms, the geology of the azure mountains beyond the red forests, the chemistry of the pre-chlorinated hothouse atmosphere and ultra-nitrogenist soils—they created a superior effigy of their homeworld inside their mothership. They developed their infantile notions of the soul from *units of soul* towards the *totality of deities*. They spawned again, explosively. Their superchitinous bodies wore thinner with each subsequent generation. Pheromone literature was on the cusp of degenerating into kitsch by the forty-thousandth generation. The Konchuu finally learned humility.

The First Masterpiece of the Marquis de Sade

Donatien Alphonse François loathed his harpsichord lessons more than any other lesson imposed on him at the Lycée Louis-le-Grand. Though he had already mastered the fundamentals of the instrument early on under the supervision of the venerable Abbé Jacques-François Amblet, he balked at performing even the simplest pieces by Rameau, Marchand, or Handel in front of others, let alone to rehearse. It was uncharacteristic of him to display such habitual cowardice over the damned instrument: an instrument that was so aggressively idiotic and favored by composers who were aggressive idiots in turn; idiots who were possessed by a moblike sense of *vocation* to attend harpsichord recitals for the sake of cultivating some remote strain of idiot joy charted only by those who delighted in it; but, especially, idiots who owned by means of formal inheritance or exploitation a harpsichord who then instructed other unwholesome, fawning idiots in the banal art of the harpsichord. Such a breed of idiot is predisposed to be unworthy of any semblance of *rank*, to be favored by God over yeast, eels, earwigs, gastroliths. When he wasn't flinching while hitting the harpsichord's keys, poltergeists would hurl the good notes and sour chords back at Donatien for hours after he'd finish practicing, regardless of how tightly he'd wrap his feather pillow around his head like a beavered helmet or if he'd raise his window in the hopes that the coming winds would drown out their clamor. These poltergeists mimicked his mother Marie Eléonore, who abandoned her wrathful child for a convent humming with the spirit of the living God; his father, the Count de Sade, who could not stand the reality of an only child when he had conceived more children elsewhere; his uncle, the Abbé de Sade, who instilled in young Donatien that virtue and decency were vulgar scapegoats, proving to him also that an Abbé seen at a brothel or clutching a depleted bottle of wine was not a display of scandalous hypocrisy but evidence of human nature *before the Fall.*

Donatien had just come out of an anti-poltergeist trance when he heard the old Jesuit marching up the stairwell.

This was a play he'd seen performed since its opening night. The Abbé would enter his dormitory and ask him how his lessons had progressed. *Bien,* he would say. *C'est très bien, mon enfant!* Donatien would then perform one-quarter of an assigned composition with competence. Suddenly his concentration would die, and his fingers would go into a frenzy, making nonsense out of the assigned piece and the very instrument itself. Abbé Amblet would viciously scold him at length. Donatien's temper would agitate further with each insult, as he'd counter the old Jesuit with wide, haughty swipes against his authority and sneer bitingly nuanced blasphemies. The Abbé would then administer corporal punishment when Donatien's curses started involving the papacy. The Abbé would brandish his long cane carved from hickory, force Donatien over the stool where he sat at the harpsichord, then beat him on the buttocks and base of his spine until the resulting weals on Donatien's body were deep and tender.

When Donatien first arrived at the school, he'd scream during the canings as though he was afflicted by an advanced inflammatory disease; but as the canings became more frequent and brutal, he found himself most often silent over the course of the punishment. Donatien's conduct became gradually worse despite the canings, so the Abbé then resorted to flagellation. Donatien's body became a pasture of welts, scabs the color of rust, and crimson serpents hewn into his adolescent flesh. The Abbé took Donatien's resilience against the cane as a sign of shame or humility, believing that he could make a good martyr if he'd dedicated himself to spiritual discipline over such jesters' foolishness.

The Abbé, however, never noticed the erections that would manifest usually towards the end of the caning; at least, the Jesuit never remarked upon them openly. Donatien was of an age where he could sustain erections and recognize that certain stimuli were responsible for his erections; yet he had little idea about what to do with an erection, nor could he coherently interpret the significance—let alone the *Significance*—of an erection.

One afternoon, after Donatien had finished the day's studies, he slipped out of his dormitory and made his way over to the grounds for a lazy stroll. Strolls were his favorite pastime, eclipsed only by horse riding. Donatien idolized each of the twelve horses housed in the stables. He gave each horse a name, no matter if the headmaster or the Abbé or one of his peers had christened the horse before he did. Donatien knew that horses were not baptized when they were foals; thus, giving each living horse—housed in stables or roaming feral in the country or wild in remote steppes and deserts—various, conflicting names over their lifespans was a logical and moral imperative.

Donatien's favorite horse he called Bucephalus, a roan stallion so short he could be mistaken for an ass at a distance. The horse was not afforded much exercise because of his stature, nor was he groomed as often as the other horses in the stables. His coat was matted, and his hooves were on the cusp of coiling. When Donatien visited Bucephalus in his stable, he'd stroke the horse's coat in the hope of disentangling the mats, never to any avail. Donatien would then stare down Bucephalus straight in the eyes. He was torn between embracing and beating the horse with his bare fists. Donatien chose to embrace him, remembering the dignity of all horses pristine and pathetic alike. Once he withdrew from the horse, he weighed options in his head for a new name for Bucephalus. After his subsequent meeting with the horse, he would refer to him as Xerxes.

Donatien halfheartedly strayed from his usual path. He approached a rosebush towards the outer edge of the grounds. The bush was haggard, but it had blossomed fully. He kneeled, the grass cushioning his white-trousered knee, and gazed at the sprawling flowers. They were arranged like plums in a pudding on the bush, but their hue was richer, more impressive than ripe raspberries. After a haphazard whiff, his nostrils flared, and he sneezed at the warm perfume. Donatien resented the way that sneezing made his lungs and throat rattle; sneezing over the roses also made him dizzy. He regained his composure and continued to admire the roses. He obsessively wet his lips, the once-chapped skin now pliant and rejuvenated, then kept wetting beyond any need to.

Some of his earliest instructions in history concerned the War of the Roses. There were no white roses growing on the bush.

The House of Lancaster, he mused, *has claimed this captivating bush for its own!*

The flowers resembled thick medals of just-butchered meat— filets of beef, rumps of lamb—and the petals felt just as damp and succulent.

The young Donatien, before he was sentenced to the Lycée Louis-le-Grand, would witness his uncle, the Abbé de Sade, order the servants to bring him slabs of raw meat—not on dishes but in their bare hands, between their toes, and in their mouths, navels, and anuses. Having seen that their humiliation had provoked pitiful prayer, the Abbé de Sade would eat the meat from their hands, et al, then manually purge the swallowed meat back into a favorite servant's mouth like a pigeon feeding its young crop milk. Through such bonding with his uncle, Donatien grew to love the taste of blood and the slimy, quasi-fibrous texture of the muscle and marble.

Donatien inspected the most alluring rose in the bush for aphids or locusts. He then parted the velveteen petals like a split pomegranate. He scrutinized at length the anthers and stigma at the pith of the flower, for the first time understanding what it meant for a flower to be alive. When Donatien had confirmed the flower's purity, he pinched the bald neck of the rose and tugged until the stem broke from the bush. The length of the stem, green as an unripened fig, was lined with ruby thorns large enough to impale a horsefly. He pricked the tips of his middle and index fingers on two thorns and sucked away the rising drops of blood. The taste of his own blood, more essential than the blood he savored in raw meat, made his stomach churn.

Donatien ate the petals.

They were only slightly sweeter and more palatable than grass. Donatien chewed and swallowed with difficulty, but his hunger was dampening. He bit into the sex organs by accident and grimaced at their bitterness. He sneezed loudly, then massaged his sinuses.

The rose was no more. Donatien felt a mounting pressure and irritation in his loins, like a fiery rash spreading through his internal organs. He became erect, and his erection grew more massive than he knew it ever could. Afraid that the old Jesuit or, worse, another student would discover him acting out such a scene, Donatien fled to a nearby tall poplar, which was situated away from any window of the building and settled beneath the shade.

Donatien took his erection in his hand and attempted to subdue it by squeezing it until his purple glans turned pale. He gritted his teeth in displeasure at first; but, in seconds, he found this supremely pleasurable. He started stroking his erection roughly. Donatien was barraged by visions of Behemoth rutting, nereid miscarriages, an androgynous Bartholomew, Christ with six sow-teats. The visions were more musical than any note he ever played on that harpsichord. Donatien spat in his hand, the saliva a foul complement to the fragrant rose. The slicked strokes became more hurried and punishing. He imagined the thorns of the rose he ate lacerating his genitals from scrotum to glans, drawing enough blood to fill a decanter.

Donatien ejaculated. The consequential ecstasy resulted in one final vision, in which his penis split into fours like an orchid, stamen and pistil rising from the gory nucleus. Donatien would paint a new rose to take the former's place.

Aphorisms in Concrete

Pittsburgh (est. 1758)—a steel reef jutting heavenward from the saline tide of a dead sea.

Pittsburgh was a spawning ground for graffiti—tags outnumbering latticed windows, pigeon nests, traffic signs, and shrubs by droves. The graffiti provided J with an education in symbols before she learned the Latin alphabet and internalized the phonetics, even as she'd uttered them instinctively as a toddler. J's education was spent in the backseat of a more-recent-than-advertised red Buick with her parents, usually getting locally-sourced-only groceries or to visit J's aunt in Baldwin for an afternoon, making a mental tally of the tags she saw around every block, under every bridge, through every tunnel. Before she learned about street gangs, she devised a system which diagnosed the artist's personality: tags more jagged and interwoven in themselves betrayed more carnal and repressed urges; those with more graceful curves and cartoonish lettering displayed more playful intentions.

J's amateur botanist father grew moss in a closed terrarium; by the time she entered school she had more practical knowledge about mosses than grasses or trees. Later, she realized that tags grew as mosses grow—in the company of shadows, even as the sun drives every speck of shadow from sight; for the shadows in which tags grow are born from human abandonment.

Burned through fifteen years—heaps and heaps of temporal ash. Haunted by *self-style* superseding *self*, being eaten, savored by a nostalgic, omnivorous world. Graffiti, however, stayed with her as much as a series of vaccines or government identification.

J landed an apartment in Squirrel Hill, able to get her fill of food and shopping within a five-mile radius most days, grateful that she lived in a *food oasis* rather than a *food desert*. J lived alone and felt obliged to be alone; the rent was low enough and she maintained her (suspiciously adequate) living quarters often enough that she grew comfortable in solitude a few months after signing the lease. Her apartment included a view of the city which she seldom took advantage of: thirty-five-story-plus corporate offices, fifty-story-plus skyscrapers ingenious as termite mounds, and talkative Neo-Gothic cathedrals that she hadn't entered since she graduated from Fox Chapel Area High.

Early July. The musk of the previous day's rain was still strong. Thick humidity pickled the air and by noon the concrete became hot as if it was deeply aroused. J clocked in at Caliban's on S. Craig St., the bookshop where she was employed part-time and was only three blocks from her apartment. J continued to treat working at Caliban's as a vocation until she graduated from CMU with her bachelor's in biology, with an emphasis on comparative anatomy, even after they cut her hours without explanation. She'd purchase books for herself occasionally, the last one being a concise yet authoritative volume on the extant crocodilians of the world with lush color photographs, anatomical illustrations, and historical depictions of crocodilians throughout; it covered much of what J already knew about the order Crocodilia and filled in many of the gaps of what she didn't know. The book was published in 1987, so the outdatedness of the cladograms in the book and the complete absence of the phrase *crocodilian genome* were inevitable.

The book made her cry at length, because a) it was quite petty to be annoyed over the omission of any talk of crocodilian phylogenetics when surely little else had changed, b) even after hypothetically earning a PhD, and even then if her focus were to shift from mantids to crocodilians, it was unlikely that she'd author or even be a co-author of a landmark study centered on crocodilians this early in her life, c) there was no telling if crocodilians would even be an object for study a century or two away.

J and her partner K were disturbingly passionate about each other for many months before J crammed for her first midterms, and they became strategically official by the end of her first finals' week.

K dropped out of her MFA program for visual art during the second semester of her sophomore year over a broken-off engagement; she could've easily been approved for a medical withdrawal instead.

K and J's admiration for graffiti was mutual. K was an active graffiti artist, priding herself on never accepting an official commission for *public art*. Her signature style incorporating elements of insects into the lettering: wings, antennae, and mandibles. K was also—her words—a "visual writer." She, however, worked primarily with collage, typically borrowing from Ernst's *Une semaine de bonté*. K considered Ernst's long-form collage to be the greatest novel humanity had ever produced; beyond its title page there is not a single glyph of text.

A typical exchange between them about aesthetics this would resemble:

> K: *So, .gifs. They're just one fragment of a greater moving image, most of the time trimmed down and looped to shit.*
>
> J: *I only think about them when reacting to shit in chats. They're not as pixelated beyond recognition anymore, but they still often look like shit. The fonts do it a lot for me. They don't seem useful at all beyond a very specific circumstance. Would you rather post a meme or a .gif most*

of the time? I know the answer.

K: *But I've been thinking about—well—what would an animated collage look like?*

J: *Would they still be collages since they're moving and all?*

K: *I'll reframe everything, darlin', and nobody else is gonna do it first.*

J: *Just you?*

K: *Fuck synchronicity!*

(*K laughs theatrically, J remains silent.*)

K: *The kicker trying to do this at all—carving up each .gif so they can be arranged in the manner of a print or digital collage without sacrificing resolution. Resolution is the big thing—the motion sequence of the .gif can be altered, of course.*

J: *Do you know much about computers beyond editing software or whatever?*

K: *No.*

J: *I don't either. You should find someone who does.*

K: *Any recs on your end?*

J: *None. I know a lot of scientists, one or two of them data scientists, but no true-blue computer scientists that I know of.*

K: *Fuck. I'll have to ask around, as much as I hate doing that too much.*

J: *You've asked around before and you got what you needed. You can do it again.*

K's current project was two years into its gestational period and counting. An overstated homage to Ernst's *Une semaine de bonté*, it was a book she affectionately but also earnestly labeled a *photographic novel* that contained color photographs of graffiti recorded across Pittsburgh city limits and peripheral suburbs and townships. The photographs of the graffiti were arranged so that they could loosely, ideally concretely, be read like a novel regardless of linearity.

J and K met at J's regular café by CMU called the Au Bon Pain—a chain, but neither J nor K had seen any other locations. They both got a caprese sandwich and a cherry Danish with a hot caramel macchiato with an iced water sans lemon. When eating out, it was an occasional ritual of theirs to deliberately order the same items to get closer to each other; this ritual was sometimes used to the other's advantage after an argument or in seasons of unchecked passion. The corporate office of Au Bon Pain claimed in every press release it took that all the ingredients used in their foods and drinks were ethically—if not entirely locally—sourced, and J and K accepted both the moral and epistemological implications of that claim. Nothing-special-sellout indie rock frothed from the speakers in sizzling gobs of sonic foam, but not loudly enough that the girls had trouble tuning it out.

J: I've been looking for internships. CMNH's waitlist is too long to do anything but give up on them for now. Dreams die sometimes and hibernate other times. I've got some leads, though. My department's helping me—bare minimum by any standard, but it's help.

K: Good. I envy you, making progress like that. You're doing the work, and you're getting actual help. I got no help. I only got *slights* and *fucking over* under the pretense of *help*. That's what made me quit, but I still envy you.

J: —I don't think you've ever said you envy me over anything, ever.

K: Saying I'm *envious* is better than saying I'm *jealous*. The word *envy*, I think, is a more tender word than *jealous*; because envy, as I've often heard and felt it, is a positive emotion conveying support for what the envious person doesn't have but wants for others. That's not jealousy.

J: Maybe—

Neither of them noticed who had finished their food and coffee first.

K was thoroughly disinterested in graffiti that did not call itself graffiti or resembled graffiti as anyone urban, suburban, or rural alike knew graffiti as it was seen or spoken about; but was rather sanitized under the umbrella-epithet of *street art* and was funded by some grant nobody should accept or the city who books unauthorized artists in the act but wants their cake (*cheesecake!*) and insists on eating it, too. K only heard the language of broken windows; images produced under the duress of jeopardized freedom in the name of a spirit liberated by no other means; criminal art installations that won't even be silenced by black matte paint.

J: How's your novel coming along?

K: Oh—great! I got twelve specimens in the past month after a dry spell that went on for a month and a half.

K pulled out a coffee-and-spit-stained manila envelope from her denim-plus-punk-band-lapel-pins shoulder bag and passed it to J. She undid the hemp coil and unsheathed the photographs. On the back of each photograph were catalog numbers and localities written in red ink.

081 5/14/15 DUQ 'HYPE NOW...'
082 5/14/15 DUQ 'MAMAFUKKA...'
083 5/14/15 DUQ 'I LUV (heart) EVE'
084 5/15/15 DUQ 'INT-TOLERANCE'

K: Notice how the t's are inverted into St. Peter's crosses and the orifices in the center of the p's and o's have shriveled up into anuses.

J: Duquesne?

K: Yeah. Here's more recent ones.

071 5/14/15 BLOOM 'DIAMATERIALIZZZM...'
076 5/25/15 CARR 'METEMPSYCHOTIC...'
077 5/25/15 CARR 'SOPHISTREAM...'

072 5/16/15 DUQ 'LEVIATHANK/YOU…'

J: They're all stylized puns around philosophy.

K: It took me a few hours to figure out what this meant, but yeah.

J: CMU alumni, for sure. At the very least attended then dropped out.

K: I don't know. The script's different. This one is ballooned up, while this other one looks like a twig. There's a signature style to all of them. I'm pretty skeptical that it's a single artist doing this work in numerous distinct styles. It's not unheard of, but multiple artists acting *in concerto* is more likely.

J: I see.

An hour and a quarter had passed, and the indie was becoming abrasive again.

K: Even with all this material, I don't know what I'm going to do about a story.

J: Why should it have a story?

K: It's a novel.

J: And?

K: People will think it's just another photography book otherwise. It's not like there's gonna be any text juxtaposed with the photos. I didn't wanna rip off Dare Wright or whoever from the start. What people think of it is ultimately not up to me.

J: Did that matter to Ernst?

K: No.

J: What's the plot of *Une semaine de bonté*? Don't wax eloquently about it, don't be vague, or solipsistic, none of that shit. Tell me in *concise, plain English* what that book is *about*.

K: —God man, fuck you.

J: Is this something you've ever thought about at all?

K: Once. Then when I finished it, I realized if I tried to work out what it was actually about, I'd be wrong. I never thought about it again, until you just brought it up; I still can't say either way.

J: This is something best worked out on your own.

K: Yeah—yeah, 'cuz it's mine.

They spent the remainder of the afternoon at K's place. K torrented a minor Godard film, *British Sounds*, and she turned it off once she noticed that J got drowsy watching it. K revived J by stroking her cheek, and J responded by grasping K's hand then caressing her knuckles with the flat of her thumb. K leaned into J's personal space then placed strategic kisses on her forehead, nose, and mouth. Fully alert once more, J snared K's mouth with her tongue during the third kiss. K clutched J's wrist until it hurt, guiding J's hand to her breast, skipping her shirt altogether—

Another noon had passed. K turned off her phone for most of the day because she had developed a mild but extremely irritating headache resembling shaving with a straight razor dry. She circled seven blocks around her place, ruminating on each inhale of the presumably-fresh air, often leaning against the lees of buildings without looking at the diagnostic signage for each, hoping no cars would start blaring their horns or a PRT bus would think she'd need a ride. She rested on a bench bearing a memorial plaque that meant nothing to her, then read the foreword, introduction, and first two chapters of a book-length critical study of the role—but also treatment—of women in avant-garde film over the course of the 20th century. When K needed a breather from the book, she turned her phone back on. The notifications from K's Instagram had exceeded the natural counting numbers. They were all from J.

The first five messages J sent were her apologizing if she ever came off as combative when K related to her progress and goals of the photographic novel. J alternately referred to *it* (being the photographic novel) as *genius* and *you* (being K) as *a fucking genius*, failing to justify why and presumably done to stoke the fires of their bejeweled love, and to preface what would come next.

The next few multiples of five played out as follows:

Messages five to fifteen amounted to J flagellating herself over her perceived inability to create visual art. Much of her childhood was dedicated to drawing pictures that both she and authority figures could admire. After she tore up a drawing for the last time, creating art was a source of revulsion. J developed a shadowy prejudice against even mediocre artists. J shed this prejudice only after she fell in love with K, forgiving even K's first death threat against her mother. She barely knew how to take good pictures on her smartphone and was in total darkness when it came to digital, let alone analog, cameras.

Messages sixteen to twenty-two detailed J's yearning to learn graffiti—the sixteenth message made known the desire, and the twenty-second message made known her willingness to beg K to teach her.

Messages twenty-three to fifty finally included replies from K. She made certain that J was serious about learning graffiti: that if she was feigning her desire to learn the art, K might break up with her; that K had never picked up a spray can but accumulated enough secondhand knowledge that she could instruct J just the same; that it was unambiguous to J that putting her freedom on the line in the name of creative expression was never a path for hobbyists, the half-hearted, the *posers* because, for pigs, gangs are their default. J was earnest and said nothing that hinted at the contrary. K said they'd go to some train tracks about twenty minutes from her place the following Saturday afternoon and told J everything she needed to bring.

K drove J to the spot. They parked in a lot in a nearby state park—the car had no risk of towing since it was still, barely, daylight. The path to the tracks was accessible by an easy trail, illuminated thoroughly by the newborn gloaming despite a dense canopy of silver maples and oaks. There were few fallen leaves on the path, nor had the leaves on those trees turned yet.

The tracks and the surrounding scenery were silent—the atmosphere of a cemetery, though temporary, as K knew that within a few hours a train would pass through again. J walked along the right rail, nearly losing her balance a few times by fault of her heavier-than-usual backpack, while K walked on top of the sleepers. The sunset was finally maturing.

K: You see that up there?

J: No.

K: Squint hard where I'm pointing. See now?

J: That's a—railcar, isn't it?

K: Yeah. It got derailed, I guess. It's standing up straight when it shouldn't, probably. They've not removed it yet. Maybe they don't want to at this point. It's been months since I first saw that.

The Mars-brown railcar was pristinely preserved after the derailment, save for the large tags tattooed on the lower halves of the hull. Like tramp stamps, the graffiti made the railcar more sensual and arresting than in other, manufactured contexts. A calculated mesh of green primary, purple shading, and azure background, the tags which read HENNEZZZY on the front and PERXXO on the reverse after a five-second squint were as animated yet compact as intestines.

J: We're gonna tattoo this train car? Even more?

K: Yup. Climb the side ladder and get on the ledge. I'll come in behind you.

They took out the spray cans from their backpacks. J had made one stencil before the trip—an anarchy-is-order—but she'd cut it wrong. K tore up the stencil in front of her. J expected her to do that as soon as she finished the stencil.

Therefore, J's first lesson in graffiti was in freehand. K told J not to worry about the fancy shit, that she'd get there with time. K told her to pick any word and visualize how it'd appear on the hull of the car. *As with drumming, I've been told*, K told J, *the idealized product lies in the wrists.*

Better than either of them expected, J had done a decent rendition of the word BRUH in red paint. For the next half hour until they had to scram before darkness fell, they tagged the front hull almost completely, J getting the hang of the art already and eager to get to the point where she could make a HENNEZZZEY-style tag perhaps sooner than later.

J began to understand the ur-symbology of graffiti: first, prodigy Neanderthals scarring the virgin Iberian cave-walls with mineralized paint—before the first modern colonizer set foot in Spain—producing the shapes of balloon-figured animals, organized quadrilaterals of unknown function or significance, and clusters of dots of equally unknown function of significance; second, the edifice of every building erected after the first ear of wheat was cut down with a scythe is a *tabula rasa* begging for some new joy, knowledge, and ruin; third, the modern city—a wilderness of business and construction, its buildings constantly created, destroyed, inhabited, and abandoned, those buildings being the loneliest entities in any city; fourth, piss—the language of animals, the boss looking for drugs in new hires uninterested in learning the *grammar* hidden within the piss but rather the *phonology* of despised substances in the piss, and thereafter prescribe the existential utility of his new hire; fifth, tags—the hieroglyphs of the American urban man; sixth, the *crime* is cutting out the tongue, burning the books of the hermetic American Alexandrian library.

Pittsburgh did not know K and J before now. Though Pittsburgh cradled them, even after they were able to walk, Pittsburgh minded its own business; K and J took advantage of that, and they had been an insular couple. Two months passed after J tagged BRUH on the train car. Now, the city wears the warpaint of their love.

K's novel—she finally decided on the title *Territory, Marked and Then Some*—got published in wide circulation but to limited acclaim. The reviews emphasized her photographic skills and almost always underscored and sometimes dismissed the novel's value as a narrative. Reading words written by others that she had never rehearsed in her head dented her ego in ways she couldn't have anticipated. She grew morose and gave up art altogether and banished the idea that she'd ever marry J.

K scored the first gram of coke she ever scored in her life. The darkness was tense and humming. While she was stopped at an intersection, the light taking an unreasonable time to turn green, a freight train pummeled past along the tracks overhead. She scoured each car for graffiti that she and J might have tattooed on them as the train receded from view. K wasn't shaken from this trance until three cars behind her blared their horns *go go go*.

K got home, refusing herself water, urination, or sleep. She unfurled her baggie of coke and, for want of any cleaner dishes, combined a heavy pinch of the coke with a heavy dash of water in a glass measuring cup and dipped a test strip into the crude mixture.

A lonely pink line.

Days before she had scored this coke, K had rehearsed in her head how composed or apathetic she'd be upon seeing the lonely pink line. She sobbed thinking of how J would feel and what she would do if she was in the same room; yet J couldn't break up with her to her face, nor call an ambulance. The fantasy of these rehearsals was rent apart, then she rolled up a pug-wrinkled five-dollar bill into a reed shape, like she'd seen in other fantasies and other rehearsals.

She lost her last virginity.

J grieved.

A week after K was cremated, every building in Pittsburgh was covered in graffiti. The previous night, the city wore only lingerie. Now it was enclosed in armor.

J: *This is the aftermath of a gang war of angels.*

She began reading the stream as she ignored cues to turn

the corner; to stop or go at the crosswalks or sections of the curb where she could get away with jaywalking; eyes squinting hard onto the path of early-onset blindness; eyes welling with tears over wishing that she and K could tag just one more perpendicular surface together, that K's family had allowed J to keep the smallest vial of ash clasped around her neck:

WORLD//WILL//REPRESENTATION//MATERIAL// IMMACULATE//DEDAUTHOR//THEIDEAL// THENOUMENA//THEIMPERATIVE//THEALIENATED// FAITHLEAP//EGO//ID//UBERMENSCH//OBJECTIVE// SUBJECTIVE...

She followed the streaming glossary across an incalculable distance until they all converged at the Steel Tower into a tag of sauropodian size adorning the post-Cyclopean lee of the building, dead in the center of the tower, J growing endlessly terrified that the aftermath of the angelic gang war was a spectacle isolated in J's wounded mind:

NNNIIIHHHHIIIILLL!!!

The Bombed Zoo

I was tending to the elephants when a child and his father approached the elephant house. The child very excitedly asked me what the animals were.

"These are elephants. Two of the adults are girls, and one of them is a boy. You see that baby one over there tossing his little trunk about? We call a baby elephant a *calf,* same as you'd call a baby cow a calf, and that calf is younger than you. He's a year old at most, and he's already that size."

"I've never seen them anywhere else! Even when I've been to the woods with my father, and I've seen things like deer and even a boar sometimes, I've never seen an elephant!"

"That's because you'll never find an elephant living in a German forest. They're native to the jungles and grasslands of Africa, and certain kinds of elephants are native to Asia—the Asian ones are mostly in India but are also found elsewhere in Asia. The elephants you see here are African."

"Where is Africa?"

"It's a great, terrible land to the south of Europe," the father interjected. "I have hunted elephants in Cameroon."

"Did you eat the elephants that you shot, father?"

"No. The meat is not good, so I was told by other game hunters and locals alike. I wouldn't have eaten such an ugly beast anyway. In these enclosures, they appear gentle and sluggish, but there is another side to them in the wild. When an elephant is consumed by some unfathomable rage—I have witnessed it, *survived it*, my son—it topples trees three times its height, and slaughters any poor living thing unfortunate enough to be in its line of sight. Our hunting party had been caught in its line of sight, and the elephant was docile moments before. It charged at us at a frightening speed, but we managed to kill it in three shots before any of us were injured. I may not have lived to call you my son had dear old Georg fired his gun even moments later. I will always say I killed that, and every, elephant for sport. It was killed for sport because it was not eaten, but the elephant's body was not wasted. I sold the tusks for a considerable sum of money."

"Why did you sell the tusks but not eat the elephant's meat, father?"

"There is a substance in the tusks called ivory. It is very precious in every part of the world. Piano keys are made from it."

"So every song is an elephant's song?"

"Yes. A very poetic remark for your age. The first chords Mozart ever played as a child to the last notes Chopin played before he spent the rest of his days confined to his bed belonged to the elephants before those pianos were ever built."

I gave the elephant-murderer's proposition some thought. It was not only true, but self-evident. Every concert hall from Berlin to Nuremberg—Berlin to Prague! Berlin to London! Berlin to Moscow!—resounded with the *poltergeist* cries of elephants. Human ingenuity inverted their ethereal bellows into music that we can weep and worship to. Yet, quite stupidly, we have lost sight of what is and is not ours.

What is to be done once elephants walk the Earth no more? How soon will the last elephant fetus slip out placenta-soaked and premature, never taking its first breath? Strings shall still resound in the halls, the forests, the streets—wind and percussion shall whine and thunder still, still. The piano! A piano is no piano without piano keys. A piano key is no piano key without an elephant's ivory. We must make do without when the time comes; but will we remain blind to the sounds promised to us by birthright? We can't be. So, we must devise some method to make piano keys out of human bones. We must refrain from repurposing bones from Aryan bodies—which must remain untouched until the second coming—but instead utilize bones that are strewn throughout the cemeteries of Hebrews, invalids and Neanderthals. Then when the first notes of the New Age of Song peal through the silence, leaving the Old Age of Ivory behind, we shall regain our composure.

And—in the distance, the howls of planes! People were sprinting, screaming, and being trampled and battered while mothers and fathers clung desperately to their children.

Transfixed amid the chaos, I realized that the Allies had closed in.

Distant explosions. The wind carried the ogrish odor of smoke towards the zoo. There was a wedge of dark shapes in the eastern sky, approaching the zoo, my jewel, at a breakneck pace. Dresden was being bombed. How much of the city was left? How many people were left to tell the journalists what had happened, to heal the injured and count the dead?

Höllenfeuer.

An orgy of engine shrieks, burning flesh, and shrapnel. Fire blossomed spontaneously and coalesced into an infernal whirlwind. The spectral death-moans of my elephants. Structures collapsed from the shock. The sludgy waters of the centerpiece fountain swallowed the body of its own marble angel. Lions became blackened bones. Flaming monkeys erased like sodium in water. Hippos drowned in their tanks. Where would the escaped owls and flamingos go? How would they breathe? Would their lineages continue? A poor giraffe decapitated by flying shrapnel.

Ode an Fruede.

I realized that all those people were smiling—cherubic joy. Their screams had the rhythm of uninhibited laughter. The corpses even bore rictus smiles, even if the face was partially or entirely burned. Those bodies resembled the clowns from the traveling circus I worked for years ago—God rest the soul of dear Young Klaus, whose every smile toward the end was the work of syphilis, buried in his motley getup to meet the LORD just as the LORD made him.

The purest smiles come from the dead. Covering my mouth and nose against the smoke, I realized that I, too, was wearing a wicked grin through my fingers. The engines of the bombers began to emit music. Those engines wailed: *Freude, schöner Götterfunken / Tochter aus Elysium / Wir betreten feuertrunken / Himmlische, dein Heiligtum.*

Phylogenie.

I took shelter in the bear exhibit. The bears had either escaped the enclosure or had been felled where they stood. The sky was an endless glacier of vaporous blood. I had not gone deaf. Through the feral flames and smoke, there emerged a chimera of all that existed in the natural world—cataloged in every bestiary and every zoological treatise ever composed by Man—flailing, roaring, its motions confused and directionless. It saw me, charged towards me, then vanished within arm's reach.

Ontogenese.

The hand of God burst through the clouds. God was holding a scalpel the length and breadth of five countries. The scalpel made a long incision in the sky. God's hand retreated with the instrument still in hand. From the open wound in the atmosphere, embryos showered down like the very bombs annihilating Dresden. The size of the embryos ranged from that of a Reichsmark to that of a *panzer.* Down came the embryos of giants, dragons, manticores, and fauns. Dresden became a ruin of unwavering fire and monstrous tissues.

Gesamtkunstwerk.

The definition of shapes and sounds became blurred and crooked, unlike degenerate Expressionist films.

Bildungsroman.

Allies on foot closed in. They found me hiding in the bear exhibit. At gunpoint, I was arrested. I never feigned ignorance with them during my interrogations. I was but a lowly zookeeper who read the *Völkischer*, I kept saying. Yet through the usual channels, they said, the determined—and my face contorted in such a way that the interrogation might as well have ended there—that I had reported two individuals, being the former rather effeminate ticket collector and the former roughneck veterinarian over how they conducted themselves when a visiting group of *Jungvolk* came for a tour of the zoo. I got praised, and I admitted that I enjoyed the praise; and, finally, that they were right that the collaboration didn't end with those two. I got the most praise in reporting one of the other veterinarians who, by a complete fluke on my part, was part of the Resistance.

Young Klaus, I pray you've watched over me through all this—one smile between us shall become two, reciprocated, in due time.

Tod.

Cooking Australia

Australia is a paradox: both country and continent; prison and haven; at once populous and uninhabitable. It is both a superpower and a footnote. A miracle and a disgrace.

Since the dawn of recorded dreaming, the Paradox's population has consumed and has been consumed. They were both *chef* and *entrée* before the megafauna vanished. The *Megalania*, described and named by Sir Richard Owen in 1859 as *Megalania prisca*, but century-and-a-half-later taxonomic revision binomially rechristened it as *Varanus priscus* to reflect its position in the genus encompassing all extant monitor lizards, was an apex predatory of the Paradox—but though the *Megalania* earned this role in the Paradox ecosystem, other animals in the same habitats filled this role just as well, such as the poster-child marsupial lion *Thylacoleo carnifex*. The length of a municipal bus, *Megalania* most likely dined on humans. However, like most of the singular fauna native to the Paradox, the humans revolted against their predator, and the reptile went extinct some 50k years ago. It is not definitively known if the Megalania was hunted or if its extinction was a symptom of friendly ecological competition; but regardless of whether the animal was *exterminated* through hunting, it must be granted that it was indeed *objectively hunted*. Paleoanthropologists have known, without much effort in the realm of inquiry and investigation, that the humans living on the Paradox used fire.

The beast was cooked. What is cooked is to be eaten. Such logic applied to potentially every known megafauna alive during the Pleistocene epoch in Australia.

The prey dreams and continues to dream even after the prey is digested and shit out. Human waste contains grains of memories from the realm of dreams. The flies that consume the dream-laced dung become intoxicated with the images of everything its originator has eaten since birth; the experience is more potent than the most concentrated hallucinogen, more affirming than the most densely-choreographed ritual that should be afforded to flies with their brief, brief lives.

Captain Cook—for he was a Cook but also a *cook*—was even more voracious than the humans who stalked and slew *Megalania*. The Captain devoured the thylacine and her cubs. He brought dogs and cats to every banquet, creatures of such *uncleanliness* that they are mortal antagonists to every *unclean* thing named in Leviticus. His legion swallowed the land itself and all that lived on it.

Conscious consumption here has a ceiling: the targeted obsolescence of a graft culture. Someone with their enteric mind "dreamed" that there were crocodiles, wombats, funnel web spiders, scenic rocks and other themes for posters. But the table was erected where gum trees weep, and the sun sowed melanomas.

Australia woke up one morning and imagined itself, then forgot that it had done so.

Enormous sections of it are still asleep. Shake an old log and twenty Australians will scurry out, suddenly having remembered:

The beaches growing louder.

The zoo-dazed kangaroos and poisoned rabbit caves.

The sheep-shearing lanolin-lathered larrikins.

Culture peeling off land like a cheap bandage on an infected wound.

The Australians were quick to roast any angry penguins they found. This was not because they prized the taste, but because they hungered instead for its absence: demanded pap, nostalgia and songs on the banjo.

There are eighteen human beings in Australia; the rest are paid actors with investments in gold.

An Australian dessert was once declared for a dancer. It was whipped and frothy, like a dying man's spittle. For the frosting, some tall poppies were milked. Sometimes it still appears in public.

And now some shuffling on the table is necessary.

Lance Adelaide.

Shake Melbourne until it settles.

Dispose of Perth with as much uranium as possible.

Sydney must be wheeled out on a tray beforehand, desperate as it is for inspection: all airs and towers. Weeping Victorian façades, like a pompous tiered cake.

Pull down your hat, be careful of the flies; and toss some chips to the gulls on your way out.

Amaterasu Overthrown

The space station *Takamagahara*, the circumference of a small spiral galaxy, suddenly became devoid of light. The trillions of passengers on the space station convulsed and wailed hideously, cursing the very light they were born under for abandoning them. Photosynthesis ceased; every tree, flower, and moss perished in darkness. The mean temperature of the space station's interior plummeted, slaughtering every organism that was stowed away in the station's equatorial tropics. The *Takamagahara*, in a matter of stellar days, was an inexorable cemetery for the open graves of billions of species.

The nucleus of the *Takamagahara* was the nest of the gods of the space station—where they created, destroyed, lounged, whored, yet never died. The gods held council, in the settled dark, to address this crisis of light-deprivation.

The council was led by Omoikane, the *ur-wise* god. The avatar of Omoikane was an immense six-lobed brain that dwarfed red giants draped in chain mail composed of a hundred thousand molten asteroids. Scrawled upon Omoikane's body was the calligraphy of anfractuous scripture composed with ink derived from crushed goldilocks planets.

"This," the brain spoke *sans* vocal apparatus, "was Amaterasu's doing. That stellar goddess, in sadness and desperation, fled the *Takamagahara* and enclosed herself in the center of a neighboring black hole called Ama-no-Iwato. After she fled, in unabashed insolence, the light that brought life to the station was sucked away. We will never be able to rid the *Takamagahara* of the stench of corpses of every conceivable form! We must lure her out of the black hole and bring her back *alive!*"

"Ur-wise Omoikane," interjected the chlorophyll-god Inari, "because of Amaterasu, not even cacti can grow here ever again. What remains of the plants that grew on the *Takamagahara* are scores of tumbleweeds gone astray. I, too, am on the brink of death. See how my branches are browning and dehydrating. See the petals adorning my skull falling off, leaving craterous sores in their wake. See my roots incontinently losing water. Every unit of chlorophyll in my body shrivels faster the longer Amaterasu cowers in the center of the black hole. I am grateful to my comrades for linking my body up to a respiratory apparatus so that I can stand before you all now. But nothing should dishonor them more than my death. Ur-wise Omoikane, Amaterasu must not simply be dragged back to the *Takamagahara* by her wrists and ankles and resume her duties as if she is innocent, as if we must perform our own duties in eternal willful ignorance. She must be tried—and Amaterasu should be executed for her transgressions against all life and every god in this chamber inhabiting the *Takamagahara*."

Ebisu, the probability-god who was a hovering maze of flesh and bone, spoke: "Inari's suggestion is *more than sufficiently justified*, ur-wise Omoikane. The net loss of species on the *Takamagahara* is, per my immaculate calculations, at ninety-eight-decimal-eight-four-five-four percent. The likelihood of the stationsphere recovering from such a loss is infinitesimal. Even if Amaterasu were to restore light to the station by her own volition or by coercion, our synchronized efforts in restoring the stationsphere would result in only about twenty-decimal-five-four-two percent recovery for at least ten million years. Even if we accelerated time, by twenty million years past, only thirty-five-decimal-seven-seven percent of life would be restored. This will, bluntly, never revive stationsphere to its former glory. *Yes. Amaterasu must be executed!*"

"Elaborating on Ebisu's point," said Inari, "even if we synchronized our efforts to restore the stationsphere, I could contribute least of all. I, more than any of you, have never been so *barely alive*."

"The soil," said the orogeny-god Sarutahiko, "is beyond rejuvenation!"

"I," said the typhoon-god Raijin, "cannot even replenish the soil with nutrients with my visceral cache of nitrates!"

"Nor is there hope for the aquatic life," said the satellite-goddess Tsukuyomi. "I cannot manipulate the tides without the aid of Amaterasu."

Susano-o, the venerable cnidarian-god, remained silent until Omoikane pressed him about his practical absence during the council.

"I cannot listen to you talk freely about murdering my sister and expect to be idle and cordial about it!" he fumed. "It is *my fault*! Amaterasu went into the black hole because I had flung a flayed heavenhorse into her dwelling as a prank. I planned and carried it out in jest, as siblings should expect from each other; but I never anticipated that she would react like this. I have never felt that any of my pranks had *gone too far*. Should your bloodlust against your own kind target anyone, may you execute me in her stead!"

"Susano-o," ur-wise Omoikane said, "your behavior towards Amaterasu was ridiculous and unwarranted; but your repentance has spared you from execution. Your sister, however—"

"—You cannot pass that sort of judgement without a formal consensus!"

"You have heard the grievances of your comrades with dire attention during this emergency council. These grievances alone are formally sufficient."

"But it is not decisive! Ur-wise Omoikane, do not debase yourself as an *ur-fool* to circumvent protocol and decency!"

Susano-o was not held in contempt for his insulting conduct.

"—Well," sighed ur-wise Omoikane, "if Susano-o says we should follow protocol *precisely*, then we shall."

Susano-o cast the sole vote in favor of preserving Amaterasu's life. Susano-o barreled out of the god-nest, barricaded himself in his chamber, and wept comets in darkness. He could not bear to witness his sister being murdered. The following stellar morning, the cnidarian-god Susano-o finally died of grief. Susano-o's body was ejected from the bowels of the *Takamagahara* without funeral rites.

"It almost seems," ur-wise Omoikane said bitterly, "that we executed Susano-o casually, informally."

"Don't feed into such nonsense," the squamate-god Ryujin said. "Susano-o dishonored us by pranking Amaterasu to begin with. His death, after all, made our consensus unanimous."

With Ryujin's words, ur-wise Omoikane cast off any remorse that haunted him after Susano-o's corpse was cast out into the void outside.

The gods of the *Takamagahara* prepared to lure Amaterasu out of the black hole Ama-no-Iwato. They caught a flock of sol-birds. sentient plasma formations that nest in sunspots. The largest tree that ever grew in the *Takamagahara*, dead but steadfast, was uprooted. The gods made a train of rosaries from the coagulated blood of departed Animalia. They harvested helium from adjacent celestial formations and forged a mirror the size of a moon. They cut cloth from dark matter. The gods hung these goods from the dead tree.

The sol-birds shrieked the name *AAA-/-MAA-/-TEE-/-RAA-/-SUU* with the resolve that their cries would never cease. The mirror was poised towards the black hole so that Amaterasu would see her reflection. She would then be consumed with narcissism the longer she viewed her figure in that mirror. The dark matter cloth was dyed the colors of her infinitely flowing garments.

Amaterasu, with immense trepidation, stuck her head out of the black hole to marvel at her reflection, the rabble of the sol-birds, and the beautiful cloth, all hung from the dead tree.

Hunters in ambush, the gods of the *Takamagahara* tore Amaterasu from the black hole Ama-no-Iwato. The sol-birds vanished. The mirror and the rosaries shattered. The cloth unraveled and the strands of dark matter vanished with it.

Amaterasu was bound, gagged, and dragged back into the nucleus of the *Takamagahara*. The goddess was tried on the spot. The jury of gods unanimously reached a guilty verdict for her catastrophic treason.

Amaterasu was dismembered and decapitated.

Once the gods had finished eating her corpse, light returned to the *Takamagahara*. But although light flooded the station, the stationsphere never recovered. The gods of the *Takamagahara* died one by one. The light left behind by Amaterasu was an eternal prisoner inside a dead husk drifting through space.

Somnii Draconis

I go to the shore to think. I go to the shore often, but it offers no insight, nor does it inspire any novel thoughts.

Here, the world is achromatic. My cell provider has no coverage out here, so my smartphone can't parasitize another second of my time. Not one second was an emergency. Huge rocks—lithified scales shed from a gigantic reptile—litter the beach as though the limestone cliffs that veil the coast were struck by rockets. The water that performs cunnilingus on the continent is gray as wintertime roadside slush, showing its true age.

Gulls soar in ellipticals overhead. They do not cry out. They are better suited to be kites on strings than the subtle heirs of dinosaurs.

(*Exponential frequency in reports of museum fossil collections on-display and off-display alike disemboweled by thieves.*)

Advertisements have made me sleeplessly paranoid. I'm possessed by extreme anxiety and sadness when an advertisement—on television, in a mobile app, or on a website, the same reaction no matter the source or content—offers my wife or my daughter more things than I could ever offer them by myself. All that I can offer them are physical goods that I encounter without being influenced by an advertisement, and I am sometimes scolded openly for it. Any aspect of an advertisement, no matter how minuscule or loosely suggestive, has the potential to inflame my emotions: the color palette of the background, objects; the absurdly hygienic bodies of the actors and actresses; the therapeutic tones of their voices, gingerly seducing the viewer into the narrative of the product's efficacy; the jingles and taglines that my family memorize instantaneously when they never bothered to memorize the current Top 40s hits, nursery rhymes, or folk ballads my father and uncle would perform in the sitting room during holidays and gatherings. Packaging is just as guilty as the advertisements. For instance, when I get my monthly refills of Prozac (40 mg. daily, a.m., taken with food, same dosage for one year and two months with comparatively little improvement of my already-advanced depressive symptoms, holding off to prove to my psychiatrist that I can be headstrong without a change in my dosage), they wrap the sick-piss-colored bottles in cellophane decorated with a spray of cartoon hearts, and the front-back label on the bottle reads, with minimal deviation, WE CARE. Subliminally speaking, the manufacturers of that plastic wrap and the drug manufacturers who decided to utilize it are feigning their concern for my well-being for the sake of profit through *argumentum ad cupiditatum*.

On one extremity of the beach, there is a billboard—a dead windup key enjambed deep into the earth—advertising allegedly cheap rates for one night (or, if convinced, a reduced rate plus reward points if one stays three or four nights in a row) at a Holiday Inn located two and a half miles down the road. I've passed this hotel before, and even though it doesn't look worth staying at even with the promotion, when I realized that these deals could expire at any moment, and there was no clear path for reimbursement should the need arise, I wept.

(*New black-market hype traced back to classical Chinese medicinal canon.*)

I wiped my eyes clean. From the other extremity of the beach, the first human I'd seen all morning was taking measured strides across the sand. He clutched a dowsing rod in his left hand. The instrument licked the air like a snake, searching out the auras of coveted minerals. Every dozen paces or so, he picked up a rock, examined it, then fed it back into the ocean.

I approached him as he made his seventh round. The folds of his black tweed coat billowed like leaves lapped by a wild breeze. It was baggy on his *bonsai* frame. From his breast pocket shot a cluster of dead yarrows. Bees wouldn't bother him much. It was a shame, though, that they must have surely driven butterflies away. He was over forty, his glasses filthy, taut lips holding back innumerable secrets. His yam-colored hair, made wiry by the alkaline breath of the Atlantic, spilt down his back and shoulders in gentle coils.

(*In which farmers upturned dragon bones while ploughing their fields.*)

"Excuse me—excuse me—*sir, I'm talking to you*—what is it you're looking for? You're prospecting? Why aren't you using a metal detector if you're prospecting? How do you expect to find anything without a metal detector? Anything!"

The man squinted his eyes like a vacuole expelling waste from its cell and replied in a sleepy, viscous voice. He sounded as if his vocal cords were an overcranked camera, or he was hearing every vowel and consonant echo against his always-pricked ears and kept stalling mid-sentence.

"You might suppose I am a prospector, at least by analogy, but I do not prospect for metals, rare or common. I seek the sex of stones."

(*The priests who received these dragon bones from those farmers would then grind up the bones and weaponize their supposed healing properties against metaphysical ailments—*chi *imbalances, dimming souls, rotting spirits left over from bygone possessions.*)

"Rocks have genitals? There are no organs at all in rocks!"

The man thrust his face into my personal space then pried open the lids of his right eye with his forefinger and thumb.

(*An Austrian-German anthropologist named G.H.R. von Koenigswald was one of the leading figures in research devoted to* Homo erectus. *Conducting further work on* H. erectus *on behalf of the Dutch East Indies Mineralogical Survey on the island of Java, von Koenigswald first visited Hong Kong in 1935 where, one day* *during his stay, he made a detour into a drugstore. He noticed a large jar filled to the brim with molars in the very back of the store. They were being sold as dragon teeth. von Koenigswald, upon immediate scrutiny, realized that the teeth belonged to a primate larger than any that existed either in the 20th century or anywhere in the known fossil record. He kept the molar in his hand and went to the apothecary at the counter and said: 'I will buy this from you. But please, tell me. Where did you find these teeth?' The hospitable apothecary replied: 'Oh, I don't go out and fetch those myself! I get shipments from all over, you see. I've been running this store for thirty years, for good reason. But those teeth, sir, were all found inside a few of the caves over in Guangxi. I can tell you're a respected scientist in Europe—do you know off-hand, sir, how many papers you've published?—because nobody else asks questions like that about my inventory. Do you know how to get to Guangxi from here? First, you must—')*

"When I consider everything about your eyes, I see that your horizon is—a horseshoe. You will say the same about the horizon in my own eyes. Physicists are sages—you're fed this all the time, but you only call them *geniuses*. I'm not interested in geniuses, you see."

(Charles R. Knight had, in dire secrecy, microdosed on fossils to receive visions which he used for reference while painting his murals.)

"You're young, but you were still born in the Century of Sages, where we've discovered that *Nature* is not merely *nature*, but the perpetual coupling of *Nature* and *Unnature*. Sage Schrödinger, for instance, in essence, a parallax of time and matter."

(For they dug up the coal and bored for the oil then sold and burned it. Though the Earth caught a fever which shall get worse until Her sweat finally breaks, nobody got even a passable high from the gasses. The ammonite's spiral eventually meets its paralleldimensional counterpart, crashing into it, fusing into a dimensionless nothing.)

"What are you going on about?"

"—Guitar strings."

(Knight's secret got out through no fault of his own. The effects of paleo *are subject to what species are ingested by the user. Sauropod-dosers, for instance, feel immense and are often found dead with an exploded stomach, the contents therein being copious amounts of coarse vegetable matter. Mammoth-dosers grow inhumanly shaggy and die from heatstroke or fur-rot. Megaloceros-dosers experience incomparable migraines, spouting and generally commit suicide by gunshot or traumatic impact. Smilodon-dosers teethe their canines on wood, brick, or metal until their mouths are nests of bloody splinters. Theropod-dosers form hunting parties during episodes of prolonged psychosis; they stalk stray pedestrians in the dark then cannibalize them, all while intoxicated on* paleo *in the streets.)*

The cryptic prospector resumed his mysterious work and intentionally grew deaf to my pleas and epithets; yet I held no sincere grudge, for he was the most interesting thing that the beach had ever revealed to me.

He then picked up a rock the size of a skull and beckoned me over.

(Popping tears of amber like birds harvesting gastroliths. The lenses in their eyes reproduce until the eyes resemble those of the arthropod prisoners in the gems. The kaleidoscope is too much.)

A trilobite was encased in the rock. It was a beautiful fossil despite the right flank being chipped off. The contrast was stark, and the ridges of the segmented exoskeleton were prominent. The compound eyes, sandpapered by the fossilization process, bulged from the lateral sides of the head segment.

The man turned the rock in his hands, examining the specimen comprehensively.

"Yes—probably *Calymene*—the fat cephalon and tricadeca-segmentation are dead giveaways."

(Ravers who ingested Carboniferous ferns were found standing dead in a christpose, having exhaled continuously until their lungs

gave out. 'Like a Roman roadside,' a forensic investigator remarked to the press.)

He set the rock back on the ground, stooped, then withdrew a mallet and chisel from his coat pockets. Jamming the tip of the chisel against an obvious pressure point in the rock, he raised the mallet and struck the head of the chisel, then again and again until it was reduced to a thick rubble. What remained resembled a pile of rotten teeth. He picked up a shard with his forefinger and thumb, then scrutinized it.

"Do you know why we know that fossils respired before their tissues were mineralized?"

"—What you just did was *disgusting!*"

"Certain sagely humans had suspected that these *sculptures* were the remains of living things since Antiquity; but when that Danish Saint-Sage matched tonguestones with the teeth of leviathans, he negated any serious skepticism against this conclusion that they were, indeed, from living things forever. Then, we drew anatomical and behavioral connections between the statuesque life of Old and the fluid life of Young; not only from the specimens themselves but from any adjacent minutiae which revealed the nature of the paleoclimate they inhabited. They are still somewhat considered 'failed sketches' in the infinite tapestry of Creation, despite their individual aesthetic and compositional merit in the Great Chain of Being. Much later, we definitively detected residual biomolecules in fossils—unfathomable organic wisdom entombed in the lithified dead. *Peace be upon* all the dead we know, do not know, will never know, have forgotten, will forget. That is the sex of stones—the sex of stones you deny so adamantly. I seek the vestigial memories locked in the fossils."

(*Regulatory bodies the world over prohibited gift shops from continuing to sell authentic fossils as souvenirs, drug-busting those who did not comply. Defunding natural history museums altogether in the interest of public safety became a general trend.*)

He scooped up the Silurian splinters and arose.

"You've looked so sick this whole time, young man."

My counterargument froze on my tongue.

(*Paleontologists=pariahs, living the rest of their days snug in bulletproof vests. Mothers and fathers of dead sons and daughters marinate livestreams and reels with bitter grief. Methodological naturalism is cursed back to the birth of Aristotle. Creationism revives in the public sphere with moral duty and pipe bombs. Families were finally able to heal.*)

"Perhaps not sick—*exhausted?*"

"Everything exhausts me—indeed."

"Things have become too complicated."

"Yes."

(*SCIENCE IS NOT AN ILLICIT SUBSTANCE read the picket signs, then destroyed along with their picketers by counterprotesters— the majority rule.*)

He places the shard of the trilobite in my hand.

"Swallow it. Don't chew. It will cure you. On three."

I didn't know what to say anymore.

"*Ichi…ni…san!*"

We tossed the fragments to the back of our throats.

My bones, becoming slurry—my limbs, receding—my mouth, shifting—my flesh, oozing and calcifying—my torso, segmenting—my pupils, reproducing asexually, rendering the world a blurry kaleidoscope—

Such vivid memories, so unlike the blind artistry of humanity!

Two young boys found a pair of human buoys, curled up like pill bugs, bobbing against the blazing dawn reflected on the water.

A Fable of Salmon

The virgin boy was invited to an orgy by two diva-esque girls. Their names were shrouded in airs of licentiousness at the only school in the endless town. It would occur that Sunday at an address he didn't recognize, hours after all the town retired from its single church with its cramped pews, tinny acoustics and sweltering heat that remained despite the ceiling fan always running at maximum speed. There would be no cameras.

Before the virgin boy received his invitation, no words were ever exchanged between him and the diva-esque girls.

Their first, and last, words to him were: "You want a *wonderful* time with us, don't you? Not just us. *Everyone's* going to be there!"

These were the only words ever addressed to the virgin that made him blush.

The boy thought of the diva-esque girls often at night when he was certain no sound would be heard in the house until the first light of dawn. During the day, he'd crush the crystals of those images, pestle and mortar, and wouldn't think of them again until night returned. He imagined their images leaving his body when he urinated in the stalls down to the last golden drop—he didn't like the curvature of the sides or distension of the bowls of urinals but liked the shifting air and shadows of bodies behind him and the squawking of clearance-sale shoes against stained tiles even less. He could only actualize *the sublime* when he thought of the diva-girls.

Yet there was purity in it. His fantasies emulated the molecular assemblage of fruit pregnant with seeds, the springtime gaping of flowers' maws, the voyages of pollen-grains and fungal spores on gentle breezes, the frenzied cloning of microbes *ad infinitum*.

Animal reproduction was filthy and invited filth. Ever since he had witnessed a pair of robins grappling in the driveway as a preschooler—twittering with sexual lunacy, flapping their wings furiously but never taking off for the air by an inch, his prudish father blushing as he told his astounded son: *they're just fighting, leave them alone*—he had been acutely horrified by the biological violence of sexual reproduction.

Yet the virgin hated that status faux-innocence. Though his aversion to animal-filth was absolute, he accepted that it was the only way to shed his wretched status. He didn't know how to weigh his options for practical scenarios to get wound up in, let alone to approach others about abnegating his virginity. When he'd think of the diva-girls, or take longer showers than usual, or unbutton then unzip his pants to urinate more openly, his mind would writhe in agony over the question of:

(micro/below-average/average/above-average)

Every inclination towards one category or the other was compromised by doubt. He looked in the mirror, always dressed, only to groom himself. Thus, comparing his appearance to others at the school led to distorted perceptions of his physique and physiognomy. Angle; curvature; musculature; the health of his hair and scalp; the prominence of his budding jawline; how robust or lacking his thighs and calves; the technical name for the hue of his irises.

He fiercely longed to take off his clothes in front of a girl; he already knew that her duty as a woman was to let him mold his sense of self on his behalf.

The virgin snuck out of his house at the first hint of twilight.

He didn't fear getting caught by his father. He was usually out on aimless errands at such an hour. The virgin presumed his father got groceries during these intervals, but the appearance of new groceries in the pantry and refrigerator was sporadic enough that cash bets on either outcome could not be made with confidence. Predictions could, however, be made about what kinds of groceries would appear without any chance of deviation.

There were enough byways and empty rooms in the house that it was remarkably easy to go unnoticed. He wanted to put on a suit for the occasion but there was no suit to be had, so he opted for a pristine white t-shirt and unshapely pajama pants checkered red and black. He argued:

(*comfort/ease of removal*)

He plugged the address into Google Maps and navigated towards the destination with difficulty, getting needlessly nervous whenever the app's false-woman-voice instructed him where to turn and where to keep straight too loudly. The route was more well-lit than he had anticipated. He never heard the barking of paranoid dogs as he walked. The rumors that there was no police department in the endless town seemed true.

The venue for the orgy was a squat-yet-imposing building tattooed heavily with tumbling and clashing graffiti. It was once a modest art gallery before the virgin was born. The space lost its grant support following unfavorable public engagement. Its contents were funneled to more prestigious galleries, and the proprietors abandoned it after nobody else made offers to buy, repurpose, or demolish it; so it stood, like an acid-rain-weathered obelisk, for eighteen years.

The doors were tall and painted brightly—yellow a truer yellow than canaries can be bred for; purple succulent a purple than Concord grapes; pink so precious a pink that no salt could bring it for flamingo or shrimp. The virgin was tall enough to reach the door handle easily. The handle was dry, but his hands were clammy. He pushed once, forcefully, then barged in.

The virgin was halted by two bouncers. They were astoundingly tall—the virgin's chin only reaching their waists—wearing well-fitting suits of seamless and imposing white. Shoes, belts, gloves, ties; the suits resembled, in essence, a land conquered by a strong blizzard. This whiteness was not relegated to their attire—their dramatically bleached hair slicked back, eyebrows plucked to match, eyeshadow and lipstick suggesting death by frostbite, and polished nails like small icicles. Flesh and clothes were synthesized, synchronized hoarfrost.

No words were spoken between them for some time. The virgin didn't know what words should be said, and the bouncers didn't know if any words should be said at all.

The male bouncer caved, then asked: "Did you come through that door by accident?"

The female bouncer added: "Did you already know, before coming here, that you were supposed to push the doorhandle instead of pulling it to enter?"

The virgin spoke for the first time since the diva-girls invited him to the orgy: "No. I was given directions by some girls at the school, and they led me here. There's an orgy that's supposed to be going on. Is this the right place?"

Female: You come here with such excitement, yet you doubt the directions given to you once you're here.

Male: Would you act the same if you were given directions to a place of punishment instead of reward?

Virgin: I don't know if I like punishment or not. I've been told I could learn from punishments.

Male: So we will make learning a punishment for you.

Female: The only thing that will save you from this punishment is what you already know.

Virgin: I don't know how much I know.

Female: Do you know the name of the organ between your legs?

Virgin: The pee-pee!

Male: You're *much* too old to be using that phrase, especially if you came for the orgy.

Female: Please use a different phrase. Something more appropriate for your age. More fitting for your intentions.

Virgin: Dick/prick/cock!

Male: Do you say these (*-ck, -ck, -ck*) monosyllables when the organ is erect or when it is flaccid?

Virgin: Hard! Always hard! My dick/prick/cock doesn't exist if it's not hard! It's not hard if it doesn't twitch like frog legs in brine! It's not hard if those girls aren't colorful and animated in my head! It's not hard if it wilts into nonexistence after I spurt carnal milk!

Female: Absolutely *vulgar*! Consider this your final guess regarding the name of the organ between your legs. Your answer must be *dignified*.

Virgin: The—penis. It's the penis.

Male: In your diatribe on how your penis doesn't exist if it isn't hard, do you know what makes it hard?

Virgin: Blood. This blood comes from the heart, and it is only fitting that it comes from the heart.

Male: Perhaps so, but for your sake, the heart ends where the erection begins. Blood! Blood is filtered through—?

Virgin: Bladder.

Male: A failure, but slight—the urine originating from the filtered blood is stored there, but it is not filtered there. Before the bladder is—?

Virgin: Tubes. A pair of them called *elopian*! Then—then— the kidneys!

Female: Yes. Back to your penis getting hard. When it's agitated enough, do you know the name of the imitation of milk that comes out?

Virgin: Se—se—se—

Male: Spit it out! Think of your penis spitting it out when you say your answer!

Virgin: Semen! Semen, semen semen, semen! *Semen*! Semen… semen[…]

Female: You are closer to entry.

Male: What is the little gash on top of your penis from which both urine and semen come out of?

Virgin: The *etheri-a*.

Female: Remove 'e', replace with 'u'. Shift place of 'r' and '-th'. Add another 'r'. Delete 'i'. You are left with? New word is?

Virgin: Urethra.

Female: Can you ever cover your urethra with the skin on your penis?

Virgin: What do you mean by that?

Male: You are closer to entry.

Female: Where does the semen come from?

Virgin: The testicles! There are two? Not three, or four, but only two?

Male: Two. How many tubes do the testicles have, so that the semen can come out of the urethra?

Virgin: Two—two?

Female: Two going without the testicles, but how many tub-ules are within the testicles?

Virgin: I don't—I thought the testicles had nothing of the sort inside them!

Male: Should he be punished?

Female: No. His ignorance of the abundance of the tubules is not criminal.

Virgin: You tricked me?

Female: We have asked you, and will ask you, every question in our heads in earnest before we can let you into the orgy.

Male: What do you know about vaginas?

Virgin: Everything I know about vaginas is that penises are meant for them.

Female: Do you know where you came from? How did you get from your mother into the world? What was the bridge between *mother* and *world*?

Virgin: Her vagina. Of course it was. But—I can't do that, get a woman pregnant. I need to get hard and spit semen without that happening.

Male: If that's what you want, what is the best course of action?

Virgin: Don't spit your semen in the vagina.

The bouncers turned their heads toward each other and redirected their gazes back to the virgin. They said, in unison: *You may enter.*

Suddenly, the beings of the bouncers blushed. Every follicle of hair on their bodies bleached white turned brightest sanguine. Their dead lips flushed with life again. Their fingernails became crimson, as though every vessel behind those nails ruptured and dyed those nails with blood, but not a drop dripped from the tapering of their nails. Their suits, gloves, shoes, and belts became that shade of hue reserved for matadors.

The bouncers stood aside, and the virgin proceeded.

There was no art on the walls, and the ceiling's white paint was faded and dirty. Drywall, insulation, and maimed fluorescent tube lights hung like bats. The virgin's footsteps echoed deeply. The tiles had shed their glaze like serpents and the raw porcelain sounded like a scratched chalkboard against the soles of the virgin's shoes. There were no cracks or blemishes in the architecture.

There was another pair of shoes in the distance, mingling with the rhythm of the virgin's footsteps.

The virgin didn't want to call out. Instead, he stood still and waited.

The footsteps grew fainter, then more prominent again. Prominent, fainter, prominent, prominent, fainter. Then they were going in circles. They stopped, then went in circles again. Then they were walking in a straight line.

The footsteps grew exponentially clearer and louder, but the virgin couldn't discern where the footsteps were coming from until he turned around.

The virgin and the orgy-goer, Benjamin, recognized each other from the school. He was a minor player on the baseball team—there were only three other teams from the adjacent towns they'd ever play against—but the only one on the whole team with glasses. He did not, however, have a blemish on his face. As such, Benjamin was inclined to insult his peers who did worse than him on exams or mispronounced technical or archaic words and expect to get away with it. Despite this, he was admired. Many students referred to him as "the cutie on the field" more than "Benjamin" for at least three semesters.

"You're here, too?"

"I was invited."

"I see. Why?"

"I don't—I don't know. They just did."

"Who?"

"These girls. They said I could have fun with them if I came here."

"Oh. I know those girls. Much better than you."

"Yeah. I—I'm sure you do."

"I'm glad you're here. I really am."

"Thank you. It's great being here."

Benjamin stuck out his hand, fingers spread apart at the maximum distance. His smile was wide and sincere; two of his incisors were chipped. The passion in his eyes made it clear that he could burst into tears at any moment.

"Please, take my hand. I'll take you to where the orgy will take place."

Dry palm in slick palm, Benjamin led the virgin to where the other attendees congregated.

"They're all from our school, aren't they?"

"Where else should they come from? It's the only place where they could come from."

Nobody had disrobed, nor was anyone even touching platonically. Some boys were leaning against the support beams, eyes downcast and thoroughly disinterested in immediate existence. Girls and boys sprawled their bodies on the floor like starfish, staring intently at the remaining light fixtures overhead that somehow still worked—their goal was total blindness. A few boys were pacing to and fro, clicking their tongues and whistling triplets without rhythm. Girls ate cooked meats bare-handedly and with grace— turkey drumsticks with black, hard skins bursting with the flavor of garlic; fatty pork ribs slathered in a glaze of brown sugar and honey and covered in thyme; grilled filets of salmon marinated in lemon juice and mustard powder; rare sirloins egregiously seasoned with black pepper and mild chilis. Boys ate fresh fruits—apples from Fiji and tangerines from Morocco; fermented bunches of white and red grapes, many of those boys getting drunk for the first time off them; grapefruits were gouged and sucked; pliant mangoes flooding with overwhelming juice; crisp green pears that refreshed their devourer with every bite.

The two diva-girls were sitting together beneath the only window the virgin had seen in the building, a single bullet-hole making a vast nerve net out of the glass that remained. Never had the virgin seen so much exposed flesh on other people, let alone on them. The diva-girls wore only matching underwear, bras and panties emerald-green. Their quartz-pink acrylic nails were of uneven length, both nails on the index fingers and pinkies chipped and broken. They dyed their hair black when once their hair was blonde. They were eating guavas, and after every bite they made out with each other without swallowing the fruit. When their lips parted, they spat out the remaining seeds onto the ground or on each other's faces with snorts and laughter.

They stopped laughing. They both glanced at the virgin from across the room. The eyes of the diva-girls and the virgin locked for ten jagged seconds. The diva-girls then withdrew their gaze and redirected their eyes to the ceiling, then the floor, then back at each other. They didn't speak, and their facial expressions conveyed a disgust they did not attempt to conceal. They resumed making their way through their guavas. They spit out the seeds without making out again.

The virgin's horror surge. He covered his mouth with both hands because he did not want to disturb the lurid peace in the room. He was the first to shed tears that night. Benjamin placed an affectionate hand on his right shoulder, massaging it, then slid his hand to the base of his neck then stroked his hair. The virgin blushed and faint whimpers escaped his lips. When Benjamin heard this, his strokes became more tender so the virgin could sigh louder.

"It's okay. There are more people here that you will couple with."

"I want *them*, Benjamin! *Them*! How dare they invite me here and then—how *dare they*!"

"*Want* is temporary, my darling friend. *Want* means nothing when *have* is actualized. Please calm down. Please wipe the tears from your eyes. Please become determined again. Nobody will want you here if there are tears on your face. Nobody will want you if you don't let go of futile desires. Believe me, they want your virginity to themselves. They pride themselves in destroying virginities. It makes them hard. It's a rite of passage. This prospect, wonderful friend, should make you hard, too."

The virgin took Benjamin's hand and Benjamin led the virgin deeper into the gallery.

"When will it start? I can't take being a virgin for much longer."

Benjamin smiled sweetly and said: "It will start soon. Don't worry. You are always on schedule to shed your virginity once you've achieved puberty. Once—yes, yes this is true—once you're able to ejaculate, once you're able to get over the initial horror of realizing that the most useful yet most useless substance on Earth comes out of your penis, comes out when urine doesn't come out. Friend new, *friend eternal*, I'm not like you. I was once, but not anymore. I've lost count of how many girls I've had, but the fingers on my hands are enough—I don't have to use my toes for reference yet. You will soon discover that you don't have to think about this in the way the adults tell you to think about it. Rather, you should listen to me, and people like me instead, at least until you're an adult and you can decide what the truth of these matters is for yourself. You will reevaluate how important being like the adults is once you aren't a virgin anymore."

"You're hiding something."

Benjamin halted, scowled: "I have nothing to hide from a friend like you."

"You've done—things I couldn't have thought of. I can't say what kinds of things. I can't say what I mean."

"Why, you can say anything, everything! There's nobody left to force you to be quiet. I won't tell you to be quiet, no! I want you to speak until you're hoarse. Yet—when you don't know what to say, friend—what you mean—say *nothing*."

"I want to say something because something is there."

"Then?"

"It wasn't just the girls, was it?"

Benjamin betrayed a doll's smile, but his eyes were still harsh, and the virgin couldn't tell if Benjamin was enraged at him or if he was about to weep himself.

"Yes, precious friend. My virginity was not lost to a girl. Perhaps that's why I don't put so much weight into having girls, but I stopped caring once I discovered how they both felt. I don't prefer one to the other. Some of the boys I've been with are here tonight. I'm still wondering if I should be with them again. Should you forfeit the idea of going after one of the girls here, try your hand at one of the boys. I know you didn't come here with that hope, that thought; but crossing the threshold of *without-thought* to *thought* leads to *intent*. Telling you about how my virginity was lost will plant seeds which will grow into *thoughts*. It's the only action that can be taken without my soul burning with regret for the rest of my life."

"Have you ever loved any of those boys? Or those girls?"

"I was taught, since I was very young, that love comes around once in a lifetime."

"Have you loved anyone?"

"—I love you!"

"—How could you love me, Benjamin? Why would you even contemplate loving me? You have only called me a friend! Am I not your friend?"

"Because I have only one chance to love someone. I chose you as my lover because I had to. If I didn't choose you, I'd never be able to know love. I can't live with such an outcome, dying without love in my heart!"

"There are so many people here. People you know better."

"My heart is open tonight and my judgment is clear."

"Benjamin, if you love me, you must never kiss me for as long as you live."

Benjamin fell silent. He cupped his face into his hands and sobbed loudly. The virgin wasn't fazed. When Benjamin revealed his face again, his expression was so distraught that it replicated the desperation of a tragic mask in Grecian theater. He balled his trembling hands into fists then let his arms fall to his side.

"I won't. I don't need to, my love. I never needed to kiss you. Your hand in mine, as I led you down this gallery in anticipation of your virginity being no more, that's enough. That's my proof, proof of my love for you. Since you don't want it, it's mine. That it's mine alone means that it's enough for me."

Benjamin's hands went slack. His tears ceased to fall. His lips and his brow went loose,

his eyes sobered again. The virgin was ambivalent toward the whole display.

"My one and only love, I don't know if I should be here anymore."

"Why would you miss out on an orgy?"

"It is more necessary for you to be here than it is necessary for me to be here. I have nothing to surrender, but you have everything to gain."

"Is this part of your so-called love, Benjamin? That you're leaving me here?"

"There is nothing 'so-called' about my love for you!"

"It can't be anything else. Those tears had no true feelings behind them. I don't—I don't think those smiles were real either. Those warm and inviting smiles of yours, so cold and repellant beneath the surface!"

Benjamin didn't ball up his fists again, but the virgin had seen such rage before only in his father when he had inconvenienced him.

"No. Not then. Now?"

Benjamin spat at the virgin's feet, missing the toes of his shoes and leaving a white frothy meteorite on the tile.

Benjamin stormed off. The virgin called after him, pleading with him to stay for the orgy, but never saying sorry for questioning his love. Benjamin turned around and shouted: "I hate you! *I fucking hate you!* I loved you once, how miserable and fleeting that time, but my hatred towards you now is *your fault alone!*"

Benjamin fled the gallery howling curses without words. Few of the other orgy-goers turned their heads at the noise, and none of them retaliated before feasting and lazing around again. The virgin was relived at first, but then he realized that Benjamin had been his guide to the orgy itself. He stood still for a while, thinking of how he'd compensate for Benjamin's departure. He started entertaining the notion that there was no orgy that night, that the school had assembled here to idle and eat fruits and meats just to make him vulnerable, that when he was vulnerable enough, they would gang up on him and butcher him on the spot. It was, however, mere entertainment.

Suddenly the orgy-goers who were reclining leapt to their feet and stood rigid. Those who were eating had spat out whatever was in their mouths, threw what was in their hands on the ground, and stomped the food into mush.

They took off their clothes deftly, but still refrained from touching each other.

The virgin's eyes darted from body to body—up/down, down/up, side/side. Internalized how different their anatomies were to his own. Erection *gorged-gorged* but the virgin did nothing. Acting then would be premature. He must see the spectacle of the orgy; how naked bodies conquered each other *en masse*.

The nude orgy-goers began to dry-heave while squeezing their penises and breasts hard without ever stroking them. They all doubled over, and the virgin anticipated group-vomiting; but they stopped heaving altogether. They all began to hiss and groan and shriek. Their spines began to shift into humps, becoming bell curves of flesh. Their skins spontaneously flushed red in horrible rashes. Their necks craned to the ceiling, froze, eyes turned upward like saints.

Their bodies stopped changing and the gallery fell silent.

The virgin had to stroke vigorously in order to stay erect during the spectacle. He had thoroughly analyzed their morphology and decided that nothing else could arouse him more ideally. He could not see the diva-girls as they were before again and expect to prolong an obsession that should have died.

The orgy-goers all turned their heads towards a corridor that the virgin had passed as he was being followed by Benjamin. They began to plod toward it and the virgin followed them silently.

The corridor led to a ballroom that was poorly lit by paraffin candles on the walls and in the remaining arms of the maimed chandelier. The tiled floor bore thick mud tracks, bruises of water damage, and faded bloodstains. It was the mustiest room in the gallery; the few windows that were broken provided little ventilation, and the virgin's nostrils and throat became swampier with every inhalation, and he began swallowing rapidly, digging at his eyes.

When all the orgy-goers were accounted for in the ballroom, all but the virgin approached the first potential mate they saw.

They considered each other head/foot, limb/torso, organs/ organs. The mates began panting heavily, their blackened tongues falling past their chins. (*Virgin grinds his thumbs against his fingers in anticipation.*) After each drew in a massive breath, they began lunging at each other (*eyes dilate*) then drawing back in a dance of hesitance. They made white-knuckled fists and boxed each other (*lip chewed*) while missing every blow. When the routine slipped up and a blow had landed (*lungs interrupt with a start*), the unfortunate mate fell to the ground. On their backs, their mouths stretched wide and cavernous, exhaling musically, hands groping madly for their lovers' bodies.

Rutting commenced.

The room was a display of zoological Brownian motion. (*No shrieks to interrupt them—*) The faces that the virgin knew in the ancient school had disappeared. (*—a spectator of bellowing flesh/ fusing flesh/flesh = like from unlike.*) Their smiles distended into snouts fitted with rows of hooked teeth. (*Limbs frozen, standing there with joy and valor receding—*) Their bellies sagged as low as their humps rose high. (*—interrogated self in tempestuous head again/again/again/again…*) Knees bent halfway towards crouching. (*…worth it/needed/necessary?*) Breasts, asses, genitals attractive in inhuman ways. (*Flee/flee/flee?*) Swagger like fish dehydrated. (*Stay/ stay/stay!*) The orgy doesn't notice that a form they once knew remains fixated. (*Lip chomped hard but never blood drawn nor sores blossom—*) The ecstasy from before is no longer, and each gesture and motion of the copulation becomes more subconscious. (—*strands of public hair bunched up/twisted/no courage to tear out to feel something.*) The voices and eyesights of the throng dissolved in the rutting. (*Where has my prick gone/had I ever a prick at all?*) Their newly sharp teeth fell from their jaws single file, their empty gums black as coal. (*I never wanted to be a virgin—*) Their eyelashes and hair shed and fell like a beard shaved. (—*losing this virginity hovering inside would kill the I the only I that I have would it?*) Blemished skin, dead skin peeled from their bodies snakelike, beginning with lips and terminating in heels, covering the floor of the ballroom like sawdust. (*I never was an I/had an I/needed an I—*) Their fingernails and toenails slipped out of their cuticle nests. (—*I lied to those bouncers out front didn't I?*) Their eyes fell from their sockets but they never faltered in speed or convention in their copulation. (*I never deserved to lose this virginity never/never/ never/never/nev-er-r-r!*) Their bones liquefied inside of them and all the definition of fingers/hands/arms/shoulders/necks/heads/ torsos/abdomens/legs/feet left the orgy-goers. (*I never even wanted to lose this virginity and I nev-er-r-r will!*)

The ballroom became a vast, throbbing pool of flesh adopting the properties of liquid mercury and amoebic sheets of sperm. The new flesh kept trying to copulate like its former inhabitants, but the new flesh kept failing.

The virgin fled the gallery.

The stars were still out. The virgin cursed the dawn that had not yet come. He felt pangs of triumph in his heart. Any foreseen punishment from his father or any disciplinary action from the school seemed inconsequential. The virgin wanted to sleep until he could witness a fresh night. He vowed to never masturbate again.

The breeze behind him had suddenly been disfigured by terrible noises. The virgin turned over his shoulder and saw the bouncers, now garbed all in morbid black, approaching him from afar with devilish speed, sprawled on all fours in a berserk locomotion that mimicked the gait of monitor lizards.

The virgin stood bravely against the bouncers once more as they reared above him taller than bears, eager to eviscerate his overripe soul from his tragically pure body.

They said: *There is no reason you should have survived, let alone resolved to flee.*

Zhuangzi in Chrysalis

The classical probability of Zhuangzi dreaming that he was a butterfly over being a butterfly dreaming that it was Zhuangzi is heads or tails. The result is, however, the same regardless of whether it is heads or tails: Zhuangzi awakens, and the dream ends. In algebraic terms, the variables x (that is, the metaphysical essence of Zhuangzi) and y (that is, the metaphysical essence of the butterfly), when added together in either order, will always equal the sum (that is, Zhuangzi awakening from the dream and wondering which possible trajectory of the dream became reality).

When Zhuangzi composed his parable of the butterfly, it is not immediately evident that he ever believed (let alone entertained) that the dichotomy between Zhuangzi and the butterfly was false; or, if he did, he concluded that it was either too inconsequential or too damning to interrogate further.

Zhuangzi/butterfly may dream of becoming *butterfly/Zhuangzi*, but those outcomes of *Zhuangzi/butterfly's* dreams operate only in the parameters of heads/tails. Should those parameters expand beyond mere heads/tails—for instance, tails/feet, mouth/hand, eye/chest, etc.—*Zhuangzi/butterfly* may become *Zhuangzi/tiger, crane/Zhuangzi, Zhuangzi/kirin, mantis/Zhuangzi,* etc., all by Zhuangzi redirecting the focus of the dream to a different subject altogether. If Zhuangzi loses control of the dream, he allows the dream to resume control. Moreover, *Zhuangzi/butterfly* may transcend the need for other living beings in the parameters altogether, so *Zhuangzi/butterfly* could become *Zhuangzi/chair, coin/Zhuangzi, Zhuangzi/stone, jewel/Zhuangzi…*

The possible combinations between the metaphysical essence of Zhuangzi and various units of the material realm are endless.

Yet the parameters under which the dream operate necessitate that Zhuangzi is the constant element of all these combinations—the independent variable. The dream never relinquishes Zhuangzi, since it is *Zhuangzi alone* who awakens when the dream terminates. It is not the butterfly, nor the chair, nor the *kirin,* nor the stone that awakens—they are the dependent variables.

Moreover, the dependent variables are fundamentally limited to the worldly experience of Zhuangzi.

Though it is not outside the realm of possibility that some intrusive element (i.e., instructions received from a deity or a spontaneous vision of the immaterial realm) may tamper with the criteria by which the independent variable pairs with the dependent variable, this is, by all worldly reason, unlikely. Zhuangzi is wise and learned in the ways of the Dao, but his knowledge of all things is fragmentary. It is quite improbable that there will be a *Zhuangzi/jaguar* or a *maize/Zhuangzi* or a *Zhuangzi/kangaroo* or a *coconut/Zhuangzi.*

Thus, the symbiotic relationship between the Dao and Zhuangzi must be scrutinized. If the Dao is evident in all things and the sage is one with the Dao, then Zhaungzi should be acquainted with everything that exists outside the butterfly. Is it that the sage Zhuangzi is not synchronized with the Dao or is the Dao deliberately withholding the totality of its nature from Zhuangzi? If the Dao is withholding itself from Zhuangzi, is the Dao conscious or even sentient?

Regardless, Zhuangzi is of the world; the Dao is beyond the world, though the Dao is its evident governor. The dream of

Zhuangzi is the nexus between the world and beyond the world.

But the Dao cannot be named! For it is the eternal Dao!

However, there is a state, though of infinitesimal duration, before Zhuangzi awakens where *Zhuangzi/butterfly* is *simultaneously* the butterfly and Zhuangzi. At once gigantic and puny, insectoid and anthropoid, mute and vocal, wise and ignorant. As there is a state where *Zhuangzi/butterfly* is both at once, there must also be a *chrysalid* state where *Zhuangzi/butterfly* is *neither* Zhuangzi nor the butterfly. Whether this state of *neither* derives from either identity being sublimated while in the *chrysalid* state or if it derives from some sort of negating nothingness, is a moot point that can be debated for eternity.

Zhuangzi/butterfly, whether they are in that *simultaneous* state or that *chrysalid* state, are in stasis between existence and nonexistence.

There is no possible end-result other than Zhuangzi awakening; but, if the equation $x+y=z$ is disrupted somehow, that Zhuangzi could become a different human variable altogether (for instance, Laozi, or Tu Fu, or Deng Xiaoping), then it must follow that the result is different. The new independent variable must awaken from its own dream, making the former independent variable and the new independent variable congruent in terms of absolute value; but what should become of the dependent variable? If the independent variable awakens, then the sum will be equivalent; but it may not. The independent variable may not remember the prefacing dream or think to compose "The Parable of *Heads* and *Tales*" at all.

The fate of the dependent variable could be total negation. Ultimately, beyond the scope of the parable itself, Zhuangzi must die. As he dies, he will cease to produce or inhabit dreams. Both the butterfly and Zhuangzi are transient, able to not exist at any given moment; only the anonymous Dao is eternal.

The Game Show Expats

Announcers, born on different days in different years in different hospitals in different countries, hosted the same game show. The announcers—all men with booming voices, scripted enthusiasm, and sanitized wit—bantered with the game show hosts—all women, deliberately—to tease what the contestants would win if they succeeded at whatever mind-bending, ridiculous task was at hand. The show— its genesis being in the meeting room of a collective of writers and producers employed by a humble film studio in Seoul which later became localized across four continents after wild popularity across Korea—combined both the novelty-game and trivia formats; versatile presentation, a refreshing aura, and sheer luck were to the producers' advantage. On September 7th, 2025, the announcers said, in three different time zones, that the on-screen contestant had won an all-expense-paid trip to the Florida Keys.

Géza the Hungarian's torso was sickeningly burnt. That morning, Géza's body was slick with sunscreen; he had learned his lesson as a child taking a scalding-hot shower after an hour and a half in the family pool on a clear day in early August. Now the sunscreen had dried up, and he lost track of the time because he was enjoying the sun, the hot Atlantic breeze, the orchestrated cries of seabirds, and ever-hissing tides. Géza knew that if he did not go back inside the hotel soon, he would be covered in blisters and his supple, unblemished flesh would scab up into plates of dead skin and dried blood; but Géza was a hedonist at heart and his heart needed the beach sun, and he was transfixed to his chair by the already deep pain from the sunburn.

Géza called for Melinda from inside the hotel room. The room—a double—was fitted with a wide-screen LCD television, a large rosewood desk, lamp fixtures beside the memory-foam beds, and a remarkable view of the seaside. This room, paid for by the game show producers after Géza correctly guessed the name of a minor African dictator who reigned in the 20th century during the trivia portion of the program, was beyond their expectations. They were in no position to protest.

Géza could have afforded this very trip with the salary his occupation afforded him. He oversaw distribution for a plastic goods manufacturing company headquartered in Zagreb but had operations in Szeged as well as Ljubljana. Yet registering as a contestant for the game show not only saved him out-of-pocket expenses but also gave him much-needed legitimacy for his vanity. Melinda, and everyone in Szeged who owned a television—not only those who were fans of the game show—tuned in to see if Géza would pull through and win something grand, or if he would make an ass of himself and return home empty-handed.

Most of his coworkers' bets favored the latter outcome; many of them lost a considerable amount of money.

Several times Géza beckoned Melinda before she came out. She apologized curtly. She had been showering, her shoulder-length dark hair and pale skin wearing thick droplets and smelled lightly of two-in-one rosemary shampoo.

"Please. Help me up. Be gentle. I've been in the sun for a while."

"My God, Géza, you're red as a lobster!"

"Those lobster tails we had last night—mmm! The chefs here did a splendid job with them. The meat practically melted in my mouth!"

"You're coming inside. Then we can talk about what we'll have for dinner tonight."

Melinda helped Géza back into the hotel room. He was incapable of lying down, so he merely sat at the foot of the bed, hunched over, careful to remain motionless. The sun permeated his entire body: his broad shoulders; his rotund, hairless belly; his taut legs; his round and wrinkled face, crow's feet sprouting as of five weeks before he won the trip; even the bald spot, resembling a canyon, on his graying head.

"Do you see any melanomas?"

Géza asked his wife even after he went on errands that took no more than an hour back in Szeged.

"Not yet. Just blisters so far."

"Oh, that would be great! *Amazing*! Our trip, our *free trip*, and all *future trips* probably, ruined by your husband getting skin cancer!"

"Don't be so sure of yourself, Géza. This sunburn may be huge, but all I see are blisters."

Melinda found an especially large blister that resembled a soap bubble. She brushed it lightly with her index finger, then stroked it as if she were stroking the chin of a cat.

"Does that hurt, Géza?"

"—Not much."

She then put her thumb and forefinger on the blister, gradually applied pressure, then let off the pressure totally. She repeated the cycle twice over.

"How about now?"

"Melinda—why do you ask?"

Suddenly, Melinda squeezed the blister with all her strength. The translucent contents of the blister shot out and splashed onto the surrounding skin. Géza howled. Falling onto the bed, he groaned and whined in pain.

Melinda began slapping and scratching Géza's burned flesh. He choked with pain, tears dousing his eyes, teeth grinding to the point of chipping in half.

"Géza," Melinda scowled, "you pathetic motherfucker. You conned me. From the moment we made eye contact, you conned me. Everything except your eyes gave me the impression that you were intelligent, more intelligent than anyone else I had professed love to before. Anyone can have your job if they're taught the right strategies. Anyone can get your exact speech patterns by reading a few books and talking to themselves in the shower. You're a *parasite of true intellect*. Deep down I always knew you were conning me. You're already making this vacation—everyone saw us win this fucking trip because of your *educated guess*—all about yourself. Does it feel good to waste years of someone's time, Géza? Surely, it does? I won't let you savor that feeling ever again!"

"*My love!*"

Melinda marched over to the rosewood desk and picked up the soiled knife resting on the dirty plate with remnants of the lobster from the previous night. She approached her writhing husband, knife poised like the beak of a heron ready to skewer a fish darting at its feet.

The beach, decorated with towering palm trees that swooned in the breeze like a heart consumed by love, was infested with vervet monkeys. The monkeys, like their mainland invasive cousin the Rhesus macaque, are Old-World monkeys that were introduced into Florida from East Africa. Florida—a biological dumping ground for voracious organisms with the privilege of feeding without natural predators—readily welcomed the monkeys into its folds, as they trod the path of the Burmese python and the snakehead fish before them. Since then, the vervet monkeys became veritable deadbeats, doing little else but loitering, breeding, gorging themselves on stolen food, and becoming woeful drunkards on fruity cocktails, straight rum, and margaritas.

Manuel the Argentinian won the trip without inviting his family over on the mainland to the Keys to visit him. His Floridian family never cared about him, and most of his extended family likely didn't even know that he existed. Manuel's vocation as a journalist for an emerging left-wing publication called *La mensajera solar* based in Buenos Aires made him a black sheep. His extended family's consensus about the Left had been informed mostly through mingling with the dregs of the Batista regime in Miami and elsewhere. Manuel had entered to be a contestant on the game show as part of a dare by the editorial staff, portraying himself as a constantly-quotable *intellectual dumbass* to amass meme-fueled publicity towards the paper.

Manuel was on the beach, wearing nothing but aquamarine trunks and orange-tinted shades, getting drunk on a helping of lime margarita. It was his third. It was midday. The two empty glasses, sticky with lime juice, salt, and Manuel's dried saliva, were littered at the foot of his lounge chair.

The heat made the tall glass he was drinking from sweat. The beverage was on the verge of getting warm. This made Manuel take larger draughts of the drink. He enjoyed warm alcohol; this made several drinking buddies gag at times, even dry-heave.

If he had his way during the taping of the game show, he'd rather have chosen Tokyo over the Keys for his trip. He could be trying hot, genuine, unflavored *sake* at the bars lining the illuminated streets of Shibuya instead of the cheap, imported swill available at either this resort or his usual haunts in Buenos Aires.

There were no other tourists in sight, but he was not alone.

After his fourth margarita, he tapped out and stumbled back into his room, miraculously never losing his grip on the folded lounge chair.

Laying down on his bed, he gazed out of the wide-open window. The horizon was wide and blurry. He sat up, too fast. When the dizziness subsided, he sauntered over to the windowsill. There were still no tourists, but there were a few beach towels strewn here and there without an owner. Once again, he found the empty margarita glasses he had left on the sand. They looked ridiculous there without booze in them, more ridiculous than a depleted beer bottle teetering over a storm drain.

He then suddenly saw two vervet monkeys rush over to margarita glasses. They greedily licked the rims of the glasses then tossed them aside. The monkeys looked hideous and pestilence-ridden to him: their gray, grizzly fur and wide, anxious eyes nestled in long, whiskered faces black as chewing tobacco.

"*Monos repugantes*," Manuel muttered.

He plodded back to the bed and blacked out face-down against the leftmost pillow.

Manuel woke up again five hours later. It was sunset, the best he'd seen at the resort thus far. Manuel opened the window and took in the ocean breeze the dusk offered to him in large, intermittent gulps. Manuel then went down to the lobby and purchased three bottles of water, a bag of salted pretzel sticks, and two bags of salt-and-vinegar potato chips.

The snacks and water kept his shot appetite stimulated while he video-called several friends he didn't want to invite. He slept again at 3 a.m., and the next morning he went to the cafeteria and had loose steel-cut oats with brown sugar and butter, two dry sausage links, and a gushy fried egg. The meal was enough to agitate his acid reflux.

While eating and belching, Manuel suddenly became obsessed with a grotesque idea. When he finished his meal, he was overcome with an implacable horror akin to an episode early in his career where he had investigated the murder of one of his own committed by a gang of neo-fascists.

He decided to go out on the beach and drink again. This time, Manuel would only have one margarita.

When the cocktail waitress brought out his beverage, Manuel waited until she was out of sight until he drew a half-full bottle of Temazepam out from the left pocket of his trunks. Manuel got the benzos perhaps too easily, but it took him two months for the bottle to be half-full. He took out four capsules—one pole white, the other red—split them, dumped the contents into the drink, and stirred it in quickly with the straw.

Manuel set the drink down on the sand then waited in the shade of a nearby palm, his gaze never losing sight of the margarita.

A vervet monkey waltzed over to it, snatching the glass by the neck. Much of the margarita spilled onto the sand, but the monkey stopped in its tracks and lapped up the remains on the ground as if it was cold rain after a long drought. The monkey coughed from an unfamiliar bitterness to its favorite drink.

Within minutes the monkey was prostrate on the sand, thrashing, seizing, jaws opening and closing like a beached fish. Then it lay still.

Halfheartedly expecting the monkey to resurrect at any moment, Manuel debated on what to do with the corpse: whether to leave it in the open air for scavengers or the maintenance crew, bury it unceremoniously, eat it without any side dishes, or burn it until the whole beach stunk. Manuel kept mulling it over—mulling—mulling—mulling it. He'd get found out if he didn't decide soon.

Yet there were still no tourists in sight, and he was unquestionably alone.

Farid the Algerian was far from a stranger to the Florida Keys. Before winning the trip on the game show, Farid visited Florida four times prior on the pretense of business. He co-founded, along with five others, a finance startup in Algiers called RexStatic. Its assets grew considerably within the first two years of its operations, quickly having heavy stakes across the rest of Northern Africa and much of the West Coast. When the firm's influence reached America, Fort Lauderdale was RexStatic's first operational branch on the continent.

Five months before the founding of RexStatic, Farid married a woman from Jakarta named Lintang who came from a line of glass artisans. They had a son that they christened Haroun, six months after the founding of RexStatic. Farid won the trip to the Keys during the game show three weeks after Haroun's fifth birthday. After the broadcast had concluded and the contestants were ushered backstage just as the audience was ushered out of the studio, Farid dialed Lintang shouting *I won, I won, you saw that just now, my love I fucking won*! Though Farid had described the Keys fondly to Lintang before, Haroun had never seen them; since it was so close to their son's birthday, they decided to make the trip as much about Farid's win as it was Haroun's birthday present.

"Haroun, it really *was* your birthday!" Lintang consoled him. "You're going to keep every last present you got, nothing's being taken away. But this isn't like any present you've ever gotten since the day you became our son. This is a trip to somewhere you've never been before—if I pulled up a map of the world on my phone, you wouldn't be able to tell me where it is on it! I haven't been, either, though I've been to a few other places that neither you nor your father has been to. He'll show us around. You're going to have more fun than you ever thought you could!"

"I—I don't wanna! I wanna stay here! I've got all the presents I need! I've never *been on a plane like you dad, like you mom!*"

"Son," Farid interrupted him, "you will love going on a flight. It's much more peaceful than even a tram or the metro. You've always told me you wanted to see the world, right?"

"Yeah—"

"These days, going by plane is the best way to do that. The only way, at this rate. If you want to see how the world is beyond Algiers, you're going on this trip. We don't have anyone right now to babysit you anyway."

"Besides," said Lintang, "you've never seen clouds up close! You'll also see how blue the sky *really* is when you're on a plane."

Haroun was well-behaved on the flight and didn't get too excited until they arrived at the hotel. Farid had been in finer hotels in the Keys; Lintang had been in finer hotels in Jakarta, even. Haroun had, however, never been inside a hotel, and initially believed that the stay was permanent and threw a tantrum over it until he was firmly told that it was only a temporary stay.

After everyone had unpacked, the family unwound and turned on the television. It was a weather forecast segment of the local news. Though the meteorologist was using too much jargon in English too quickly in a Transatlantic accent for the entire forecast to be understood— Haroun was essentially hopeless in comprehending the forecast—the animated pictograms corresponding to certain weather patterns and remembering that Americans used the Fahrenheit system of measurement made the forecast comprehensible enough. For five days of the week, it'd be sunny and clear with mild breezes on three of those days. The weekend would be cloudy if not overcast, but there would be no precipitation all week. After the forecast ended and the regular news took over again, Farid changed the channel to cartoons per Haroun's request. Haroun was used to seeing these same cartoons dubbed into Arabic, and seeing beloved characters act out their scripts in the original English, which he didn't know a word of, made him bawl loudly. The television remained off for the rest of the afternoon.

They ate breakfast in the dining hall at 6:30 a.m., a half hour after it opened. At 8 a.m., Farid and his family were taken three miles up the shoreline via Uber until they reached a small dock. There were only a few boats; evidently it was privately owned. They were approached by a tall, middle-aged man with a salt-and-pepper beard that reached down to his deeply tanned navel— exposed, as with the rest of his wiry-haired torso, through an unbuttoned denim shirt—with enormous thighs and calves past his green khakis and a Panama hat complete with an emu feather that had lost almost all of its barbules. On all five fingers of each hand, there was a duplicate of the same stainless-steel ring with the same faux-elaborate cross design in the center. If he wore a cross around his neck, it was totally obscured by his beard. His shades were tinted pink, but Farid could still not discern the color of his eyes.

"Ain't this a fine mornin'," he said in a manner reminiscent of how Farid heard Floridians living in or near the Everglades talk on YouTube documentaries about the local impact of invasive species. "You're Farid, who I spoke to yesterday afternoon?"

"Yes, sir. You're Samuel?"

They shook hands. Samuel's palm felt like the skin of a bullwhip, and he shook Farid's hand with the force of a piston.

"I do hope that your flight from *Owl-jeers* went smoothly."

"It did, indeed. That was the little one's first time on a plane, and it was smooth for him, too."

"I tell you now, I wish I'd got on a plane before I was grown, let alone a young'in. I've been on planes since, and I've seen more places than maybe I ought've in my whole life; but if you can take a young'in on a plane, you should."

"We made a good decision bringing him along," said Lintang.

"This is the *surprise* part of his birthday, yes."

"Well, happy birthday, young'in!"

Haroun shied away from the man in shades being so friendly with his father over seemingly nothing, but not once did Haroun cry in his presence.

"Just gonna be y'all three? Still gonna just take it for a day?"

"Yeah."

"Four-fitty."

"It's fine if we do FrancaWallet, right? I don't have that kind of American cash on me, and I realized as soon as we paid the Uber that my checkbook's still in the hotel room—my apologies."

"'Course it's fine."

Farid paid Samuel and Samuel gave them a tour of his boats. Out of the four that were available, Farid picked a standard Hurricane-brand deck boat with a purple awning. Though Farid knew how to operate a deck boat on a rudimentary level, Samuel walked him through the controls and basic safety protocols out of compliance and goodwill. After Lintang had applied a head/toe coating of sunscreen and insect repellant on both her and her son, Haroun was the first to receive a complimentary lifejacket and disposable earplugs from Samuel.

Farid leisurely took the boat out a mile and a half from shore. Haroun disliked the noise of the motor at first but grew accustomed to it. Farid stalled the boat and removed his fishing rod from the holder mounted on the gunwale. Farid never caught any fish in the Americas, but Haroun had seen him catch saltwater fish before. He was also less certain what kinds of fish might take the bait. Though he'd always hoped to catch a swordfish or marlin as soon as he learned how to fish in his youth, he knew upfront that his first catch would be a dwarfish, borderline inedible fish that could almost satisfy as a snack.

Four lines were cast out into the water, but nothing bit the hook. Haroun, meanwhile, was fixated on the splendid, raging dance of the water's surface. Lintang was lounging in her seat in a canary-yellow one-piece and a wide-brimmed straw hat indulging in the fierce sunlight.

Twenty yards from the vessel, Farid saw an opaque, gray shadow lazily drifting inexorably forward beneath the surface like a drowned corpse caught in a strong current. It was an oblong shape with a square head terminating in a flat, broad tail resembling a lotus leaf.

Haroun went over to Farid and asked: "Do you see something out there?"

Farid pointed out the shape. "You can see it?"

"No."

"Look closer to where my finger's pointing."

"Oh! It's a mermaid! A *mermaid!*"

"Shh! Haroun! You'll scare it off!"

"—But it's a mermaid, right?"

"There's no such thing as mermaids, Haroun. People only see and fall in love with mermaids in the fairy tales we read you sometimes when you say you can't sleep. That's a manatee."

"*Manna—tea?*"

"That's right. That's not a fish out there. It's a mammal. Mammals are things like cows and goats that have hair and make milk for their babies and for people to drink. That's a mammal that swims—you've seen videos of seals and walruses; those are other mammals that swim. But the manatee is in the elephant family instead of the seal and walrus family. You'll understand why when you're older—yes, when you're older."

"What does it eat if it's all alone out here in the sea?"

"Oh, it eats plants that grow underwater. There's grass and weeds down there, but it's tall and it sways to and fro, to and fro, to and fro like trees bracing strong winds."

"Do people eat them?"

"Do—*do you want to eat them?*"

"No—no—what does its face look like?"

Farid took out his smartphone and pretended to get frustrated while pretending to scroll and push the correct buttons.

"I can't show you its face on my phone. We'll have to get a closer look at it."

Farid revved up the engine and maneuvered over to the manatee so Haroun could get a look at its face.

"That's not a mermaid at all!"

"Oh my," Lintang interjected, taking off her shades and squinting at the animal from a distance. "It's so ugly it's pitiful! I'd rather walk through a subway and never take a train for a week straight!"

Through the water, Haroun could see the manatee's snout and noticed that the nostrils were sealed over by flaps of skin. The flippers—massive concrete oven mitts seemingly devoid of the capacity for motion—looked far too dense in Haroun's eyes to support a large, floating animal underwater for any reasonable amount of time. The manatee didn't have much in the way of eyes, just black holes that seemed drilled into the skull after it was born rather than the eyes being already nestled in the orbits at birth.

Farid crouched and put his hand on Haroun's right shoulder.

"Son," Farid began, "you're due one more present to celebrate your fifth year of life."

Haroun's eyes beamed.

"The manatee is not a mermaid, but do you want that manatee to be your brother or your sister? If not so close as a brother or a sister, at least a pet? I can make that happen. I've raised you to believe that a father—*your father*, Haroun—can do anything."

"—*No!*" Haroun screamed in his father's face without intending to. "You can't get that thing out of the water. You can't! You can't bring it on the plane! You can't feed it grass from one of the meadows or farms! Let it be in the sea, dad! *I've had plenty of presents this year!*"

"Fine, Haroun. Quite fine. This is the first time I've ever heard you say you've had enough of anything. This is the first thing you've ever said that will prove that you'll become a proper man—in due time, due time. Now, I'll teach you what it means to reject a living thing."

Farid revved up the engine again and steered the boat fifteen yards away from the manatee.

"Are we going back to shore?" Lintang asked.

Farid suddenly swerved back around in the manatee's direction and floored the accelerator.

"*What are you fucking doing?*" Lintang shrieked.

After the first jostling bump, Farid veered the boat around again, growing ecstatic upon seeing the manatee bearing a huge, bloody gash on its dorsal side which nearly clove it in half, still floating lethargically as if nothing happened. This next hit to the manatee inspired Farid to do donuts with the boat propeller on the manatee. Within seconds, the animal's insides became its outsides.

"You killed it! Those things are endangered, you told me so! Are we going to wind up in some fucking American prison because you killed that thing? Answer me! *Answer!*"

"We're too good for prison, Lintang. We're too upstanding."

Haroun was paralyzed except for the tears tumbling down his face.

"Haroun—your tears tell the world that you're still a boy, but your silence proves that you'll become a man—sooner than you could imagine."

Before the adrenaline could set in, Farid threw Haroun into the water. He could hardly swim but he frantically tried to get away from the gore rising out of the manatee's corpse. It was the first time he tasted blood.

Farid rushed to the cockpit and swerved away from his drowning child. "*Our child! Our fucking child! Murderer!*"

Then Farid redirected the course, Lintang trying to wrest him from the steering wheel all the while and floored the accelerator.

(Title card. Upbeat theatrical music. Continuous applause. Lights. Close-up.) Welcome one and all to [the game show]! I'm your host— [XXX]. This is a show, a one-of-a-kind show, that pits mind and body against matter and facts! We're going to have a lot of fun today! Alright?! (Applause again, shorter.) And now, please welcome our first contestant! From—

Romulus Craved His Mother's Milk

The workers, six days after arriving at the site, succumbed to collective amnesia. They forgot the nature of the assignment that had brought them out to the site. They forgot the name of the company that employed them, the location of its headquarters, the euro amount attached to their stipends, or even if they would get paid at all. They wore uniforms, so they reveled in the security that no man in their party was an outsider nor could be. The men forgot their whereabouts: how close or far they were from Munich; if they were still within Germany's official borders or even historical or folk borders; if they were German citizens or residents at all; from there, where they were even born or when.

They toiled aimlessly and ceaselessly in a quarry that was getting broader and deeper by the day, failing to expose any materials worth extracting. They forgot what kind of materials they were supposed to extract, and the sound of the voice who gave their verbal orders or the style of the penmanship comprising the written orders that bade them do so.

Surrounding the quarry was a forest of primarily spruces, ashes, and beeches growing in such height and with such density that the forest *ate light*. Rising above the forest was a great mountain, whose colloquial name the workers forgot; but they would never forget how virginal-and-deathly white its peak was, or the inexorable shadows it cast, or how often that mountain deprived them of the sun's warmth even at its noontime zenith. A few kilometers away, there was a river that never displayed any signs of life. When the day's work concluded, the amnesiac workers would plod over to that river, boil its water in a large tin pot—the only one they had, which they also forgot how to wash—and drink until they were pitifully nauseous. There was nothing in the forest or in the river for them to eat, or they forgot what can be edible and what is outright inedible. The workers made it back to their camp before the harsh night set in. They would repeat this cycle the following day, forgetting even more.

There were five of them. There may have been more present before the sixth day. There may have been machines, too, but all the workers had to call their own were shovels and picks that were getting caked and dull. Even so, those shovels and picks were used to their greatest extent; digging in that quarry without aim or ambition was one of the few things the workers remembered how to do, or that the workers remembered at all.

They partially remembered their names.

Hans was the only worker who remembered his proper name. His blonde beard was long, and he couldn't stop stroking it compulsively, sometimes twisting strands of it into crude braids or ripping small, frayed tufts out of the beard altogether. His body was prone to trembling while at rest; but during the day's work, his body was steadfast.

Fischer could only muster his surname. Fischer was short, his belly distended and his limbs taut. There was not a blemish on his skin nor a follicle of hair on his head. Fischer's teeth were stained, blackened, and broken; and when he spoke—which he hardly did—an atrocious miasma would billow forth from his mouth, which would occasionally make his own nostrils twitch and his eyes furrow. During the day, Fischer only worked with a shovel and was never seen using his pick in any situation. He would shovel tirelessly in the same spot each day, his hole reaching depths of three meters or more. Memorizing when sunset was imminent—transcending the need to rely on the blackening clouds, the gradual dying of the sun's light, the deepening saffron-orange of the sky, the vocalizations of certain insects and birds that were deaf-mute during the day—he'd rise from his hole and quickly reinstate every pebble he'd excavated, tamping and smoothing the earth with the flat of his shovel. He'd reenact the same digging routine three meters down at the same constant pace the following day.

Hein— remembered only the first half of his name. He was the tallest but also the thinnest of the party. Hein— had no eyebrows, coiffed hair slowly losing dimension, and a broad, poorly-groomed mustache destined for asymmetry in the coming weeks. Hein— used only his pick; rather than do legitimate work with it, he used the tool as a melee weapon against the rocks in the quarry. Half the time he'd shadowbox with the pick, bringing no sword but rather peace; the other half he would strike the rocks in warlike maneuvers, damaging the rocks beyond redemption, bringing no peace but rather a sword.

—helm was all that he could recall. The shortest and oldest, —helm bore decades of blemishes on his face that ranged from skin-popping scars to witch-moles. He was polydactyl on the left hand, his extra thumb jutting out from his primary thumb like a budding polyp. His manner of work involved digging half a meter down into one hole and then digging half a meter down into another; then, he'd take shovelfuls of earth from one of the holes and fill it into the opposite hole. —helm would do this, even well after sunset, until he was certain that all the earth from its original hole was back inside of it. He'd groan like a grieving elephant deep into the night if he so much as suspected that a single grain of one hole's earth was in the other hole.

—au— knew his name halfway. He was the only man in the party who could be called beautiful, let alone likened to official portraits on legal tender or paintings of any number of male deities from Antiquity—yet his eyes were dim, his lips perpetually pursed, his hands constantly making fists and relaxing again. —au— was a thoroughbred idler, looking seldom at the earth beneath the soles of his feet and most often deep into the forest that never moved with the wind and at the sky which was never truly clear. His idleness became so disciplined that he was finally alienated entirely from the work he once compulsorily performed with the others, even as he watched them mindlessly perform their duties.

On the ninth day following their amnesia, the five workers realized that their tasks were becoming more difficult to accomplish. Though they drank deeply from the boiled river water, they had neglected to eat still for want of edible things nearby. They'd lost about 7 kg each, or more, over the course of those nine days; their muscles succumbed to terrible cramps, and they grew exhausted well before sunset.

Fischer was the first to realize that their routine had to change so they didn't die in the quarry. A quarter of a meter into the hole in the same spot he was digging, he suddenly refilled the earth therein and went to another, unclaimed spot on the north end of the quarry to dig. It could very well have been —au— 's spot; but —au—, of course, was idling.

Fischer got down to a half-meter deep when his shovel struck something that felt and sounded unlike the surrounding rock. Clearing away more earth revealed the cranium of an apparently inhuman skull. Fischer beckoned the rest of the party over; even —au— took an interest in the discovery. Though there was no speculation whatsoever as to what terrible species this skull belonged to once and how the skull itself got into the quarry, the consensus between the five workers was that the skull had to be exhumed from its matrix.

The workers focused their collective shortened attention on one explicit task for the first time since their amnesia.

Besides the gash made in the frontal bone when Fischer

initially struck the skull and another, deeper gash in the right maxilla made by Hein— during the excavation, the skull of the animal was pristinely intact. It was a bovid, but it was not a cow that was fed by this country's pastures. Its horns were broader than any bull's and the orbits were of wider diameter, too. The skull itself was too heavy to lift, so it remained *in situ* after the excavation was complete.

—helm tried naming the creature but could only muster the syllables *au—* and *—rochs* and *—rochsen*, separately and never together.

The five workers, feeling the approach of the setting sun once again, sat in a circle in the quarry to ease their bones and muscles. They did not speak to each other, nor did they make eye contact while in that circle, and remained utterly motionless—except for their eyes which, when they were not blinking, were all hypnotized by the bovid skull. They took in the prominence of its zygomatic arch, the dent of the molar bone, the length of the premaxilla, the egregious injuries inflicted upon the skull with the workers' shovels during the excavation. They stared at the skull for half an hour until muffled, pounding drumming and tuneless, constant fluting emanated from the skull until it consumed all other sounds and became the *only possible* sounds. The hearts of the five workers swelled in ways they hadn't known since before their amnesia, before they bathed in the first merlot shadows of the womb, before the bearer of those wombs were housed in wombs themselves.

The cacophony ceased abruptly. The five workers keeled over, groping the dirt and gagging on thin air. The only one to vomit was —helm, but he vomited little, and his vomit was clear as spit. A short while after —helm got his vomit out, the workers stopped gagging then began to inhale and exhale deeply in unison.

They remained in a circle, but now maintained eye contact.

Their hands spontaneously traced lines in the air with their index fingers, with the deftness and precision of a calligrapher's brush. Though the workers had never seen one another perform such gestures since their amnesia—or, likely, before—they gradually recognized the symbols as they would appear on papyrus or clay.

What came from Hein—'s hands was a sequence of two symbols: a vertical snail shell and a lollipop. The symbols originated from a basal tongue devoid of vowels in its writing system, which was spoken in the far southeast, in a land known by several names but the most-oft-pronounced named was Canaan, Canaan, Canaan. Their meaning, together, was *voice*.

Hans' hands formed seven symbols—familiar to all the workers, for they were in the letters of their domestic tongue. Those letters spelled out S-A-N-G-U-I-S.

From —helm's hands came but one symbol. It resembled a spade facing downward, or a uterus bearing only one ovary. This lone symbol, used in a southern land where the whiteshining tombs of its kings took longer to build than all its villages, did not need to be spelled to have its meaning deciphered: *life*.

—au— signed two symbols, one of which was the same second symbol as in Hans' S-A-N-G-U-I-S, and the other was a horseshoe. Together, they meant *the first and the last*.

From Fischer came six symbols—again from the familiar domestic tongue—which formed a word that the other four workers had certainly encountered and used before their amnesia but was spelled differently, although Fischer's word meant the same thing. After *B-R-O-D-E-M*, Fischer formed *B-R-Ā-D-A-M*; regardless, designating *breath*.

The five workers never formed a single sentence with their symbols, or even a sentence fragment. Only the same symbols came forth *ad infinitum*, their bodies wholly devoted to the task. Their eyes stopped blinking; their mouths were locked shut as their tongues were welded to the roofs of their mouths; their blood and bowels froze solid; their hearts themselves stopped beating and their brains themselves went dormant. The five workers were like dead trees whose branches still swayed with every breeze.

Then the first organs to hesitantly revive were the workers' hearts. As their hearts beat faster, their hands slowed; and the more their hands slowed, their other organs revived in domino fashion.

When the workers' hands were finally free from the tyranny of their symbols, they moved their hands to their groins. They sank to the ground, first to their knees then prostrate, writhing and screaming like a cicada brood even as they vomited profusely from the agony. They yanked down their trousers and exposed themselves to the gloaming; their penises grew expeditiously until they were three meters in length—coiling and thrashing on the ground like disquieted cobras—and their testicles drooped down to the size of flounders. When their penises and testicles had ceased growing, their hearts were beating more fervently than they ever had during the days' work.

The primordial bovid skull presided over everything and intervened in nothing.

The five workers' now-abominably-long penises were flaccid, seemingly to the point of functional uselessness. From their massive urethras leaked quarts of a foul fluid at some intersection between pus and semen. They were yet incapable of sitting upright; they fondled their new penises—hot to the touch, but hot like L-handed-faucet tap water and unlike frying grease—in the attempt to resuscitate them and get whatever remained of the foul white fluid out of them.

When their penises finally became fully erect again, they were now the length of *zweihander* from tip to base.

While the workers were learning to walk again with their new surplus weight, —au— kept staring at Fischer and a new anger towards him mounted. Fischer had stolen —au—'s spot and consequently unearthed the bovid skull. Fischer was able to steal —au—'s spot because Fischer still considered him to be an idler, and one can get away with anything against an idler. —au— realized that, had Fischer left well enough alone, the bovid skull would never have been unearthed and the workers would have gone about their usual tasks interrupted only by death among them.

—au— took his penis in his hands and charged at Fischer.

Fischer was struck in the gut by —au—'s penis and was pinioned against the north wall of the quarry, the impact making small debris shower down from higher up the quarry onto both Fischer's and —au—'s heads, all of it bouncing off without any pain felt by either. —au— began shouting at Fischer, without syllables at first but then it was clear that —au— was pronouncing "A-Ω! A-Ω! A-Ω!" Fischer, of course, retorted, with "*brādam! brādam! brādam!*"

Hans, Hein—, and —helm looked on at this display, not out of horror, or even interest, but out of dewy-eyed stupidity.

Fischer got sick of hearing —au—'s tirade that included only syllables and lacked words, so Fischer maneuvered his penis so he could perform a glissade down —au—'s penis, strike —au— against his temple to the point of bleeding and wrest himself free as —au— staggered backwards, howling. When —au— had recovered, Fischer expertly performed a barrage of broad moulinets against —au— before he could properly counterattack. —au— fell square on his back, shielding his tear-drenched face and mouthing "*mise-mise-miserere!*"; but before —au— could finish the fourth syllabic plea, Fischer, wielding his penis like a mace, bludgeoned —au— mercilessly until his body was a mash of mulched bones and fountained blood. Much of the face between the brow and upper lip had caved in, and the jaws were contorted at the hinge so that his mouth now resembled a waxing crescent. The torso and abdomen were so battered that the nipples and navel were split by spilt gore.

Fischer, goresoaked and triumphant, rose and addressed the

three remaining workers: *"ven-ven-vi-vi-vi-vi-vid-vid-vid-ven-vid-vi-ven-vi-vi-vi!"*

Neither Hein—, Hans, or —helm understood the significance of Fischer's address; nor did they feel grief or anger looking at —au—'s destroyed body. As their impressions of Fischer before their amnesia were nothingness, so did their impressions of Fischer after their amnesia become nothingness as they witnessed Fischer murder —au—. Hein—, Hans, and —helm did not want to murder Fischer in turn, but they did not want to accept them in their folds again.

Hein—, Hans, and —helm pointed their fingers at Fischer and shrieked in unison: *"exeunt! exeunt! exeunt!"* Upon hearing their edict, Fischer's penis went flaccid. He strenuously clawed his way out of the quarry. Fischer did not take —au—'s body with him. Then, with his flaccid penis wrapped around both shoulders like a yoke, he trudged into the light-eating forest guarded by the Babelesque mountain, never to be seen again.

But even after Fischer was banished from the quarry, Hein—, Hans, and —helm did not feel camaraderie toward each other. They felt neither bloodlust nor brotherhood; only tolerance, which was wearing thin. They, too, wanted to get out of the quarry, away from —au—'s ghastly corpse and the bovid skull that should have always remained in the earth, even if they would never again savor their former memories.

Hein—, Hans, and —helm glared at the bovid skull. Their penises were still erect.

The three workers, suddenly possessed by an earthmover's rage, wielded their penises like their pickaxes and struck the bovid's skull over and over. Once the skull was cleaved in two, the world was plunged into an irrevocable night.

Baron Munchausen's Suicide

(Manuscript found crumpled in the seat of the chair at Baron Munchausen's desk, shortly after his subordinates realized that he had disappeared after retiring from his duties the previous night.)

Gentlemen! Friends, dear friends, only friends, who shall arise from your burdened bodies with arms locked in arms towards the gilded highlands of God's Heaven! Adversaries, wicked adversaries, only adversaries, who shall with grudges locked in grudges hurtle down to Hell's endless jungles of towering briars! Let it be clear, from the shortest knoll of the Alps of Switzerland to the ever-pouring mouth of the Egyptian Nile, that I, Baron Hieronymus Karl Friedrich von Munchausen, am dead! I was not so cowardly bushwacked by the Russians, or perished in a duel that would've been needless if not for my honor; nor did I succumb to tuberculosis or dysentery, or even absentmindedly drank water from a well contaminated by cockatrice venom. And I *certainly did not* depart from my mortal post in this glorious empire by "natural causes," a euphemism by which the esteemed physicians of our time might call an unexciting and unheroic death. If only von Haller focused less on contractions of the muscles and more on Satan's maladies!

No! All who read these words, all who read such words aloud, all who will hear my lamentations from beyond the grave! I was vanquished in battle, but so singular a battle in my century-long career, between *me* and *myself*. The only sickness I succumbed to was that of irreparable melancholy; the only cause of death was that of my own hand!

I, Baron Hieronymus Karl Friedrich von Munchausen, have committed suicide!

I resolved to commit suicide after a flurry of events instilled within me an *infernal* desire to die!

So! It all began after the deaths of my two sons, Johann and Erasmus, legitimately brought into this world by my legitimate wife Jacobine. Johann—the papers reported this tragedy as accurately as the gossip afforded—was torn apart by a two-headed eagle two hours after he was born. Erasmus survived him for five years, then drowned in the Seine after a canoeing accident; he was already an expert in the art of canoeing before his first spelling exam, making the loss of Erasmus even more regrettable.

(Erasmus and Johann's respective demises are exaggerated greatly. Though neither son survived past childhood, Johann lived to the age of three before contracting pneumonia. Johann was never threatened by an eagle with two heads, or even with no head, let alone one with only one head. Erasmus lived to graduate from his third year of primary school but was run over by a passing carriage while being delinquent with other schoolboys.)

Then came my divorce from the Baroness Jacobine Munchausen.

(He was never divorced from Jacobine nor anyone before or after her.)

We'd quarreled day and night since the fifth anniversary of Johann's death. This quarreling came to a head when the Baroness cuckolded me—with an Ottoman sultan no less!

(They were a happy couple that never quarreled, openly or privately. The Baroness indeed cuckolded the Baron, not with a sultan, but rather

with a Russian general. Though there was no evidence that the general seduced the Baroness for the sake of conducting reconnaissance, the Baron accused him of spying anyway. The Baron called it "spying" so the affair itself could easily be hidden from scandal. This was also why the Baron spared Jacobine from any charges against him or the empire. The Baron had the general publicly hanged the following afternoon. The gallows cleaned up, the Baron and Baroness remained happily wed and never spoke of the incident again—even when the Russians decried his extrajudicial judgement against one of their generals in the strongest possible terms, stoking the fires of war again.)

After the (*fictitious*) divorce, I went to the Black Forest to hunt, to distract myself. Five hundred paces into the trees, I came across a stag the size of a rhinoceros. Its pelt was yellow like a polluted street, adorned with imperial purple spots. On its head were terrifyingly lofty crimson antlers shaped like tangled roots. Its eyes, the circumference of Chinese jade dishes, glowed brighter than torches. The stag came towards me and began reciting velveteen, baroque words fit for a heretical liturgy. I do not remember all of what that stag said since, before it could finish its horrible tirade, I shot it between the eyes. I hauled the stag's body back to the palace by its ankles. The stag was roasted, and my men and I feasted greedily upon it; but the feast only lasted a mere half-hour, when a stag of such stature should have afforded a feast of at least an hour and a half! I was brimming with woe over the whole affair. When I had my bowel movement the next morning, I wept as I beheld the meagre, pinecone-shaped turd in the chamber pot.

(The Baron ventured into the Black Forest to hunt for the sake of leisure, true enough; but the stag he describes above predictably belongs to the annals of his fabulous madness. The beast he brought back to the palace was a common roe deer—a female hardly three weeks in age. The Baron demanded that the troops feast on the fawn. They shouted such epithets as "ludicrous," "unhinged," and even "treacherous" for expecting a sizable congregation of fortified warriors to have their

hunger satisfied by a measly fawn. The company refused. While the Baron initially threatened to execute some of the them for being "traitors," he was enough of a pushover to respect their just grievances. Afterwards, the Baron made his Portuguese cook prepare the fawn just for himself, and the Baron consumed the entire animal down to the bone and gristle alone. The next morning, Baron Munchausen was discovered weeping over the chamber pot; but it was not over any perceived symbolism imbued in the contrarily massive turd nestled at the bottom. It was known throughout the palace that he had been constipated for at least two weeks. The Baron had also lamented that his external hemorrhoids were flaring up again.)

The following day, I consulted my personal accountant about the status of my fortune. The accountant—an Ottoman deserter who previously handled the salary of a sergeant—told me, verbatim, "[you] are a destitute noble who, at this rate, can transition seamlessly into the leprosy-stricken misery of commoners." Suddenly ashamed of the luxury surrounding me my whole life, I became a beggar on the streets of Hanover.

(The Baron's accountant was not a vagabond Ottoman, but a minor Austrian aristocrat who graduated from the University of Vienna. The Austrian's calculations did not correspond, naturally, to the Baron's claims. They were, in fact, my own. The Baron was richer than ever. Moreover, he never became a beggar. He merely took strolls in plainclothes and pranked commoners with intimate casualness: many "good mornings" and "how do you do's" escalated into rough handshakes and pats on the shoulder. When he retired from these excursions, he rested his head on his pillow stuffed with grouse and pheasant feathers like every other night.)

I was saved from being a beggar through the miracle of indentured servitude under the dove's wing of a Siberian princess.

(See above. If anything, Siberian royalty would be servants to the

Baron with his wealth and territory.)

But! The princess grew tired of me. My servitude was cut from seven years to seven days! She declared me mad, I proclaim, just like everyone else!

(*This is the only claim in the entirety of the Baron's suicide note that holds one irreducible atom of weight, let alone truth.*)

So! I became a stowaway on a merchant ship *en route* to the Germanic colonies in Africa, and when the ship's captain found out that I was none other than Baron Hieronymus Karl Friedrich von Munchausen and heard with sympathetic ears of the misfortune that befell me, he persuaded the local officers to give me exclusive dominion over cotton production across a sprawling acreage of savannah.

(*There is no record or even rumor of this.*)

But! I grew bored of it all and decided to ride a ten-meter-long albino crocodile across the Nile back to the motherland, swinging my cutlass over my head and shouting *Ave Maria* till the clouds retreated all the while. My steed never ate, drank, grew tired, or bucked like the horses so beloved by all Eurasia do, for crocodiles subsist themselves off of mud—I believe Aristotle drew that conclusion; but since natural philosophy has come a long way since Antiquity, and as far as my voyage mounted on such a creature suggests, crocodiles might as well subsist themselves off thin air. In fact, I took cues from this romantic and trusty crocodile and held gulped air in my lungs to save calories and stave off the need to drink. Along the way, we slew scarabs the size of ploughs, carnivorous camels with devilish fangs, filthy ibises with rapiers for beaks, Ottoman soldiers bearing rifles that never depleted rounds—all of them felled by my massive cutlass, gifted to me by Napoleon Bonaparte on behalf of a duke who I never even considered a close friend, which never grew dull no matter how many strokes were made against the enemy! Once we reached our destination, the crocodile laid six diamond eggs before it humbly departed back to Egypt. Though the diamond eggs were, quite annoyingly, very hard to crack, the yolk therein was so nourishing that I felt that two decades were added to my lifespan—that was the last time I'd speak too soon about anything!

(*This tale is so characteristic of the Baron's fabulous madness that any further comment is just as senseless.*)

And! Should anyone doubt the episode of traversing up the Nile, or anything else I've said or done inviting raised eyebrows or suppressed chuckles, I say with unfiltered sincerity that I am as honest as an earthworm and as sane as a monastic!

(*This is the most brazen lie the Baron has ever told.*)

Exhausted with adventure and destitute of morale and pride, I decided to end my own life! In secret—secret no more!—I recruited a British mercenary who frequented a brothel, quite familiar to me, near the palace. I bribed him to stuff me into the gullet of a cannon and shoot me to the face of the moon. By the time you read these closing remarks, dear mourner, I will be little more than a heap of bones picked clean by moon-peasants, the refuse of my being thereafter dumped into the cold trough of one of their marvelous canals. So! Goodbye friends and adversaries! When you look at the moon at night—whether waxing crescent, waning gibbous, full, or nothing at all—forget not the incredible exploits of your Baron Hieronymus Karl Friedrich von Munchausen!

(*Not only was the Baron never shot out of a cannon to the moon or even over the fence of a corral, but he was also discovered alive, basking in the sun with his trousers off while humming a medley of marching songs, minutes after the initial discovery of this manuscript. Though he will not die as a suicide as initially he planned—or, more accurately, constructed an elaborate yet painfully childish chivalric tale around—he will, however, die in an alpine asylum for the insane.*)

The Revelation

Every unnatural light that was manufactured to counter the tyranny of the Great Smog over the corrupted atmosphere snuffed themselves out in unison mere seconds after the conclusion of the summer solstice.

The ensuing chaos was colossal and unforeseen. Of every noxious, glass-splitting utterance laden with the certainty that *humanity will never know another photon again*, nobody could discern one obscene utterance from another, nor ascribe them to any face, real or hallucinated. Architecture, geography, space, gravity, and autonomy were entirely deconstructed conceptually, while Death was granted some exercise in the streets again. Cannibalism became self-defense.

Five weeks into the New Black Hell—before the survivors had even thought to develop their own capacity for echolocation—a contagious idea spread unspoken over the Stygian world. This idea, a gamete burrowing itself into ovulating brains, matured from a mere idea to a zygotic desire and then into an embryonic Will.

A Will—*to see once more*!

Two hundred years into the New Black Hell, the surviving lineages of The Last Solstice scarcely resembled their ancestors at all.

Their bodies had shrunk to one-third the scale of their basal stature. Their new goatmilkwhite skin was taut and blubbery. Their toes sprawled. Their fingers fused. Their mouths shriveled. Their metabolism chilled. Their eyesight diminished to one-fourth functioning capacity. They developed two pairs of long, graceful plumose antennae fitted with hooked sensilla that granted their wearers defined pictures of their environments through sensing shifts in temperature and wind currents.

These were the inheritors of the New Black Hell's lithified darkness. The Last Solstice was no longer recalled by living memory.

Four hundred and ninety-nine years into the New Black Hell, after the young troglobites attempted a loose form of civilization again, every deliberate motion of the planet's surface came to an instantaneous halt. Every clouded eye on Earth was turned up to the sky in lunatic stupefaction.

There was, for the first time since six seconds after the end of The Last Solstice—*light!*

The new light was, at first, distant and suggestive on either side of the equator and in either hemisphere. It resembled a *tint* or a *bruise* more than legitimate *light*. This bruise was cobalt blue in color and displayed itself scattered, like an archipelago, in isolated fragments throughout the Great Smog. The cobalt bruise didn't alter its shape or luminescence for weeks; while many of the troglobites had already been crippled by hysteria, the rest grew accustomed to this atmospheric formation in the Great Smog, even *delighted* by it.

The first month after the arrival of the cobalt bruise concluded, and the *bruise* spread further and further in the sky until finally it became a *shine*. The cobalt shine singed off tufts of the Great Smog above; and, as the shine grew broader and brighter, larger growths of the Great Smog dissipated, eaten alive by the luminescent interloper accumulating power and annexing territory in the once-obsidian sky.

After three months, the Great Cobalt Shine devoured every cubic meter of the Great Smog. The sky behind the destroyed Great Smog was not blue, like the Shine that vanquished it, but a searing white—whiter than the blubbery flesh of the troglobites or any of the artificial lights that existed before The Last Solstice; whiter, even, than the brightest limestone Earth could ever muster, or the light of Polaris in the far-distant North of the Old Sky.

Thus spelled the end of the New Black Hell, and the advent of the New White Dawn.

The despot of the New White Dawn was a cobalt sun. It was hotter and twice as large as the yellow dwarf Sun which ruled the Old Sky, and the light which exploded forth from it was a sensuous magenta.

The troglobites, beholding a star for the first time with the suddenness of a newborn's crying, writhed and seized beneath the magenta light dyeing the New Sky like decapitated serpents. Millions died from unbound agony in hours, but those that survived were paralyzed by an internal super-eruption of ecstasy, orgasming constantly and endlessly until the worldwide wails of antediluvian pleasure died down and the whole planet was vacuum-silent. The troglobites, rendered breathing corpses, took root in the soil like corals until they would eventually putrefy and bleach.

All the eyes on the planet fixed eternally upward at the New Sky, the cobalt sun charring the troglobites' flesh. They saw, in a span of no more than one hour, the flourish of magenta light recede, an ebbing solar tide. The cobalt sun molted its rosy corona, and the star could be scrutinized for days without the observer annihilating its sight. The planet's surface temperature never waned.

The cobalt sun suddenly shivered and shifted. The star was fissioning, like amoebae, then it excised itself, from itself, cytokinetically. The resulting second sun was not an exact replica of the cobalt sun but was instead colored conifer-green, its light a sickly urea-yellow.

The two suns became three, weeks later. From the conifer-green sun was born a cinnabar-red sun, its light an eerie and oily sea-urchin black. Over the span of six months, the three suns became six. The cobalt sun bore another offspring, an almond-brown sun emitting a frail, frayed mossy light. The cinnabar-red sun bore two offspring, the firstborn being a dim amethyst sun veiled by a scintillating, snowy corona and the runt being an ashen-gray sun which bore a dazzling cardinal-red corona but emitted light that was practically invisible.

Six finally became twelve. From the ashen-gray sun came triplets—a *sakura*-pink sun emitting wine-dark light, a porcelain-white sun whose corona was a ring of crushed shadow, and a citrus-orange sun bearing a corona the foul color of bile. From the amethyst sun, two—a bronze sun with a corona of iron and a lavender sun with an iguana-green corona. The last of this generation of suns was born from the almond sun, an imperial purple sun emitting light that was pink as a tongue.

It took three centuries for the New White Dawn to be governed by a junta of twelve stars. By the first hour of their reign, the troglobites became an overdue nothingness.

The Twelve Suns gathered around the world in an ellipse. They waltzed slowly without an audience to ever behold them. Over millennia, the orbit of the Twelve Suns became shorter and shorter, until they circled the world at a breakneck pace, blurring and crashing into each other. The New Sky was destroyed by its own suns.

The world was not engulfed by the Twelve Suns. It became the Thirteenth Sun.

Fluora

I survived long enough to meet Fluora. She hated her real name and I learned to imitate that hatred. I had known her for only a week; she is no longer in my life. Fluora could reside in a different state by now, even in a different country; a country I may have heard of but couldn't point to on a map, or a country I may have never heard of and trying to point to it on a map would be a wasted effort. She could have a family; one she'd be on speaking terms with. She could have *started* a family, too. She could conversely still be addicted to solitude as recluses like us are prone to be. I could be a footnote in her mind, yet she is a formidable presence in my own. I don't believe she is dead yet. I think of her laughter compulsively. With each phantom breath of laughter, I repeat: *Fluora is alive and well.*

A few springs ago, I was transported to a hospital in Columbus after a suicide attempt. Before I entered the intake room where I met Fluora, a nurse snidely remarked while I was on the gurney that I looked like a minor. I was not that young, and people who'd say that I looked younger than I actually was would never infantilize me that much. Then, spitefully, I wondered if she had ever laid on a gurney for the reason I did before her.

Fluora was in the middle of an intake interview with another nurse. She was weeping worse than Jesus Christ. The noises she made drowned out all the questions asked by the nurse—a young Vietnamese man who spoke with curtness but compassion—who reined in his own volume trying to console and soothe her. She gradually calmed down and started using syntax again. The nurse's chart was full of essential notes for her intake so he took his leave, exiting the room through a door that locked automatically behind him, and could only be opened again with a badge ID or from within.

Fluora—said like *flora*, spelled like *fluoride*—was quite thin. She could rightfully be called lanky. Were there deeper implications to her thinness, just as there were deeper implications for own my thinness when I was a minor? Fluora's skin, white as a panda's fur, was pocked with small moles without any coherent patterns. She had the face of a ferret. Her nose supported a visibly worn pair of horn-rimmed glasses and from her head exploded sandy hair with curls like an agitated tide. She wore a purple pajama top with a cartoon dog printed on the chest and pajama bottoms checkered red and black. They had not yet given her the proverbial non-slip socks.

She wore that outfit over the entirety of her stay. There was a washer and dryer on-site, but she never took a change of clothes. Whenever she took a shower—over that week I knew her, she only took three showers, all clustered towards the end of the week—she came out dry in the same pajamas. It occurred to me that she chose to keep wearing this same outfit out of security. If she were to request a change of clothes from the plexiglass-bordered nurses' desk, which anyone in the ward could do without reproach, her recovery would drag out further because she wouldn't feel secure in the new clothes. I understood; at times I didn't feel secure even after I welcomed a change of clothes.

I already knew you were beautiful, Fluora, because I couldn't let you start weeping blood.

Fluora's tears had dried, sticking to the bags underneath her eyes and her cheeks like sap. Her first words to me were: "I'm sorry you had to see me like that."

"You're fine. You're quite fine. I hope you're gonna be ok."

She was flattered. This was certainly the first time she'd smiled in that facility since she arrived. How did she arrive here? By ambulance, like me? By the grace of someone else? Did she muster the resolve to drive herself?

Another nurse came—an older woman with a cache of melanomas on her face—and took Fluora away. I thought, then, that I'd never see her again, never even get the privilege to learn her name.

I was held there for another five hours. An old woman with PTSD claimed she was transported to the wrong hospital for two of those hours. I know its name by heart: Riverside. If Riverside was not the subject of one sentence, it would find its way to become the predicate of the next. After they took her away, presumably *en route* to Riverside, a man with the physique of the Minotaur and road signs tattooed all over his arms told me that I had landed in a *shithole*. The hospital wouldn't admit him over conflicts with his insurance. There was a spat between him and the same nurse who interviewed Fluora. The Minotaur tried frantically to arrange transportation for the next fifteen minutes. Eventually he booked a taxi and left the building. He didn't wish me a 'Godspeed' or a 'good luck' or anything. It was at least warm enough outside to wait for a taxi with uncertainty of when it'd arrive and not shiver.

Then there was G—, who came in after the Minotaur. He was a scarecrow with wild eyes, a messy soul-patch, and a faded, ballooned face tattoo on his cheek that looked like it was done in someone's kitchen. He kept alluding to, without bragging or elaborating further, some trouble he got into or will get into. This trouble probably wasn't petty. Instead of talking, we watched the late-night basic cable programming on the television encased in a plexiglass shield so that patients wouldn't break the screen or rip the television off the wall altogether. *How precious is that television to them?* I thought. *Precious enough*, I reasoned, *to protect the welcome distraction of one patient from the psychotic rage of another.*

After two hours of watching television in practical silence, the fluorescent overhead lights began to irritate me. After a while, it felt like large centipedes were grilling in my brain. I thought the hospital staff were conspiring against me—to put more centipedes in my brain to cook, or to take the cooked centipedes out of my brain and eat them with citrus drizzle, butter, and root vegetables.

I pounded on the window of the staff office like a cop. The nurse who answered was the same nurse who interviewed Fluora. I berated him about the duration of my wait, then he sheepishly replied that I would be seen soon. It took another two hours for me to be interviewed by another nurse who was misshapen and condescending. Everything I told her was a casual reality for me, and she cut the interview short before I felt I'd gotten into the meat of the intensity of my mood swings, the extent of my delusional thinking, much of that. I learned later that with what was revealed in this interview alone, they originally intended me to stay at the hospital for two weeks—twice as long as any of my previous stays.

It was two a.m. before I was sent to my room in the ward. I felt the exhaustion of a tick after a feast of rich, indulgent human blood. I hadn't eaten since my failed attempt, but all the staff felt like giving me were meager snacks before I finally slept at perhaps three-thirty.

My room was more spacious there than I was used to in hospitals. It was, in fact, more spacious than the bedroom in my apartment at the time. Hospitals normally resembled my lay conception of prison; but this hospital was *inviting* which, in hindsight, made it the most sinister hospital I had ever been to.

I woke up to a nurse marching up and down the hall yelling *group time, group time*! The sun was barely out. I had a strong headache because I hadn't taken any Abilify for over twenty-four hours. I presumed *group time* meant *group therapy*. I skipped group time because I was fucking miserable from the headache and waited for the staff to bring us down to the cafeteria for breakfast instead.

We were ushered single-file down a few flights of stairs and then taken along some hallways and through doors protected by barcode access. There were more patients in the adult ward than I had expected. The line of us went back twenty feet or so. The cooks were friendly, at least cordial, and offered us extra portions upon request. When we sat down and ate, conversations were awkward and banal. I didn't see Fluora.

That breakfast was the best hospital food I ever had.

When we were taken back up to the ward, I went over to the group room and watched television. I hated television, but like every other hospital, the only books they had were coloring books and KJVs. A pandemic was unfolding. Public places were being locked down, and the news station was about to give tips n' tricks on how to stay physically active during this lockdown after the commercial break. I wondered seriously what sort of hell I'd got myself into and how much worse it would become once I was discharged.

The next day, when I caved in and decided to do group therapy, the nurses made us sit at a far, even distance from each other. They didn't give us masks, though masks were already being worn on television.

I saw you, Fluora, and was overjoyed. They were giving us our medicine, which would be changed for both of us the following day.

"How did you sleep last night?" you asked.

"Like shit. I always do."

"Same."

"Do you have dreams, though? I don't."

"Not often. When I do, they're nightmares. This didn't happen last night, but sometimes they make me scream, but after I wake up screaming, I can't remember shit about them. It's like—fucking pointless, right?"

We snickered.

"Your tattoos are beautiful."

"Thank you! I did them myself!"

Fluora was two or three years my junior, but she was already an accomplished tattoo artist—steady with the hand in a mirror enough to tattoo herself. One could trace her growth as a tattoo artist between one tattoo and the next. The worst piece was a faded, blown-out spider on the index finger of her right hand—no way that one wasn't her first. The best piece was a ram's skull on her chest. I imagined us tattooing each other past midnight when the rest of the ward would stow themselves away in their rooms, attempting to sleep, picking old scabs and making new ones, astral-projecting while awake, manic bodies animated like chase-scenes, hesitation-chewing their lips and wrists, carving out the callouses on their feet, quietly or loudly hallucinating, failing to make it to the toilet on time, trying to loosen their molars, reliving divorces and resisted arrests: above all praying to be discharged whether they got in voluntarily or pink-slipped.

On me: A detailed vampire bat head on my neck. The kanji for *bloodbath* beneath my left eye. Knuckles blacked out except for radiant crescent moons. A stork carrying a baby-swaddle pin-cushioned with arrows on my right thigh. A stylized ouroboros encircling each nipple.

On you: Flower mantises on both hands, symmetrical. A ferret across your stomach. Orpheus facing Eurydice on your legs, serenading her. I'M HERE in dense script crowning your forehead.

There was a woman in there who we mutually disdained, Fluora. What was her name? She dressed like a mutilated mattress and her face was marred by terrible alcoholism and addiction. In group time, she'd always introduce herself as a recovering alcoholic and addict. After the third time, it became obvious she was bragging about what shouldn't be bragged about. She referred to you as the name you hate—the name I hate just as much.

She called me *Nero* because he was her Antichrist. She tried to convert us every six hours or so. Once, I told her that Nero didn't feed his lions enough, then she shoved the ward's only Bible which she kept hogging to herself in my face, as though she was punching with it, and told me that I had to accept Christ *now*. I snatched the Bible from her hand and threw it across the hallway, bouncing off the windowsill at the end of it. I said: *You think He'd let me do that shit? Huh? What now?!* The nurses separated us and disciplined me for disturbing the peace of the ward more than she would ever retaliate against my apostasy.

I told her, four days into my stay, that she had issues with control. She agreed, almost instantly. She asked me how to solve these issues, with complete trust as though I was one of her addiction counselors or her Christ. She still likely devalued me beyond that—and you, Fluora, through guilt by association.

Spirituality seemed irrelevant to you—and, for you, it was allowed to be.

She was not the only person in that ward who tried to convert me. Initially, I had no roommates, but I was assigned one midway through my stay. He was an effortless slob. I wonder, even after more than two years out of that hospital, how he got away with being such a slob in a hospital setting. The few times we conversed, he was always the judge for my damnation. As I tried to sleep, even in the daytime, he would masturbate in the opposite bed with excess lotion. I never protested, never opened my eyes or moved even a toe. I instinctively knew that I, myself, would be safe despite him masturbating; which meant, also, that since I kept quiet we were never separated. It made such grotesque sounds that they were overpowering. I kept envisioning the churning radula of a gigantic snail.

I also kept quiet about it around you, Fluora.

The meth-addict father! I forgot his name, too! He had what I had in his head, and he wasn't much older than me. How did he know where my hometown was? He said he always drove past it on the way to Florida. The gashes he made in his wrists healed terribly, scabbed in such a way that it was obvious the wounds weren't allowed to breathe.

When, once, me and the meth-addict father were alone watching carbon-copy reality shows in the group space, he told a story that could've very well been *the last straw*. He'd been delivering medical equipment for a couple years in Dayton. After surviving a maze of road closures, he was forced to take a tumbling-hilled backroad surrounded by farmland. A vicious downpour brought on night early without stars. A motorcycle—what he called a crotch-rocket—that he couldn't have heard come up behind his van against the rain suddenly passing him in a sickeningly wide arc from the right. He couldn't even blare his horn at the cyclist before he sailed over the oncoming bend, got bashed against a willow-trunk, and sailed another ten yards before being buried beneath his bike. The meth-addict father immediately put on his hazard lights, clumsily parked the van in the ditch, and pulled the cyclist out from beneath the premium-gas-and-rubber-stinking husk of a machine. The cyclist's head nearly dangled off a broken neck, and when he tried to resuscitate the cyclist, his hands sank into his crushed chest so deeply that he could've torn out the cyclist's heart, lungs, and esophagus with one hand. He couldn't drive anything larger than an SUV or drive even in drizzling rain again.

I told you an abridged version of this story. You cried over my abridged version more than I cried over the full version.

Then that old man whose mind was now nothing and would never return. He was formally anonymous to everyone except for the staff and was otherwise only characterized by violent outbursts. He never acknowledged you, so you were safe from him. The meth-addict father was going to strangle the old man a couple of times in front of everyone, but he refrained because he reasoned somebody with nothing in his head wasn't worth a felony, thinking especially of his daughter. Watching his daughter learn and grow was perhaps his only pride.

You knew one of them, Fluora. Mister Beckett taught you Ohio history your sophomore year, the semester that nearly killed you for the first time. You didn't recognize him until he sat at the same table as us during lunch and asked: *Remember me?* I never expected you to be downright beaming if you ever recognized any of the other patients; you were adamant, however, that he called you Fluora instead. You and Mister Beckett went up to the line cooks together and asked for seconds of poached eggs and Belgian waffles; you had, gratefully, enjoyed eating again. You went pale upon seeing that the pinky on his right hand was severed at the knuckle. His ex-wife had cut it off during an argument about their financial situation, then burned alive a tegu they adopted together—the very tegu who had its own tank in his class, which every other Friday a student was allowed to feed shredded rotisserie chicken to decompress after tests. That night I grieved on his behalf and puked to the point of thinking that my stomach was dissolving into itself; but you, Fluora, had a dream that you called wonderful, and you thoroughly entertained Mister Beckett for half the day.

Some days at group time we could request songs that would be played through a Bluetooth speaker, and other days a young music-therapist who was quite obviously an intern would come in and play simple songs on guitar and sing them. When the woman with the guitar came in, someone requested "Hey Jude". She began playing, and midway through the second verse, I was suddenly washed in grief over nothing and wasted adrenaline. I excused myself and didn't return. The moment I realized that PTSD wasn't reserved for discarded veterans or kidnapping victims was during a previous hospitalization when an elderly woman was describing how she'd piss herself whenever she caught a whiff of peanut butter because it was also her abuser's musk. You had it too, Fluora; but you taught me that our minds' erasure of brutal memories was its own form of suicide prevention.

The meth-addict father sat next to me at lunch that day and told me that he couldn't listen to Bonnie "Prince" Billie's "I See a Darkness" again because he was blasting that album in the van that night; but he was bewildered and disturbed that he could loop Johnny Cash's version for a solid hour, even when distinctly hearing Will Oldham's backing vocals, and feel cold and quiet.

We kept each other sane, Fluora. You said so, more sincerely each time. I wanted to be close to you when we got out, as close as however close would be proper. We could finally tattoo each other. When you had an extreme anxiety attack, and they rammed a needle in your ass to sedate you, I waited for you to revive in the group room, then I consoled you. I wanted to go beyond words and hug you, but you disliked human touch. Should your brain have never erased brutal memories, your relationship with touch might have been different.

At the last lunch we ever had together, I told you that I loved you. That was the only time I was able to tell you, and that was the only time you could smile at those words.

Though we always looked forward to getting home, there was one patient we met who would remain perhaps indefinitely. Her skin was more wrinkled than unironed dress shirts and she didn't have a tooth in her jaw. She'd sing songs that nobody but she had heard before; she sang, and laughed, more than she talked, because singing and laughter don't require words. She'd ask daily about the status of her discharge paperwork. The nurses would always tell her *soon honey, soon*. Turns out this woman was homeless; no surviving family, and numerous attempts to arrange transportation and finding a vacancy at a shelter had fallen through. She didn't know about the administrative politics behind the nurse's desk, and she smiled with certainty that she'd be discharged that day, or the next few at least, every time the nurses told her the same thing. The day I was discharged—you remained, Fluora—one of the last sounds of the ward that I heard was a fucked-up, half-right rendition of the chorus, only the chorus, over and over, of Merle Haggard's "Okie from Muskogee."

Hellenic Dropout

Covering my entire torso is a partial ink reproduction of the Infernal panel of Bosch's *Garden of Earthly Delights*. It is the only tattoo I have and the only transmutation of my flesh I am willing to indulge. My ears are also virgins to the piercing spike—when circumstances present themselves, I will even refuse surgery. I got it done because I had the means and the desire; there's little else to be said about modifying the human body.

My Helltorso is the subject of much gossip in Bucharest. In the more licentious quarters I pass through on my night strolls, I still get stopped by *curvă* I've paid for and forgotten—as if we were intimate outside of a professional context—asking about the meaning of the Helltorso with artificial and exaggerated curiosity. If their pimps don't tell me to fuck off if I'm not going to pay for their girls, then I tell the girls to fuck off themselves. They get furious and call me a *pizdar* or a *poponar*. I resume my stroll as if nothing had happened, the prostitutes' shouts waning in the night as if they were the hallucinated humdrum of poltergeists. In daylight hours, at cafés where failed businessmen and successful poets share space in synchronic camaraderie, girls from across the room eye me nervously. Not just Christian girls, but Roma and Muslim ones, too. Eyes of every color you could catalog in the city have eyed me with a brand of trepidation typically reserved for pathologists discovering a new disease. Crones cross themselves and usher their bodies—limbs and backs bent like the countenances of developing fetuses—hurriedly away when they pass me on the street. Once, as I was spending too much on pastries and not enough on coffee at the dingiest café in the city, I heard a mother say to her daughter: "That is Alin and he has Hell on his chest. When he dies, his coffin will be inverted like they did with people destined to resurrect as *strigoi* in ancient days. He is even abhorred by stray dogs. Don't go out at night, or he will find you."

Despite my Helltorso, my body was not up to par with my ideation. Bosch's demons bulged on me; my pectorals resembled budding female breasts, and my belly was an amorphous, sagging mass without definition. Three years of bulimia got my body down to a suitable weight so I could get the tattoo without looking wholly ridiculous. This resulted in withered tooth enamel, myriad cavities, and ulcers. My teeth are now mostly gone or artificial. I couldn't convince my mother to pay for implanting gold teeth.

"Alin," my mother would say after every extraction, "how could you do this to yourself? You are better fed than many people. We taught you how to take care of yourself. Your father would be ashamed."

Crossing myself invertedly just to agitate her, I would always reply that God filled me with demons and I had to vomit them up. Even after I got over my bulimic tendencies and paid for *curvă* whenever I liked, prostitutes filled me with melancholy because I was liberating them sexually, but I was only enclosing myself in a sexual prison. I attempted numerous workout regimens, but I couldn't dedicate myself to any of them. My diet got worse whenever I quit.

I asked friends who were keener on drugs than myself about dealers of more precious substances (pariahs gravitate towards other pariahs). There was one recurring name. Mihai was good friends with this character. He went by Tsuu, but Mihai asserted that I call him Tsubasa for the first few deals. Tsubasa taught Mihai the Japanese language, which explained why Mihai's spare time was consumed by translating children's *tokusatsu* shows for Romanian fansub websites. Heinrich, that shining German who

132

loved knives and the botany of aquatic plants, was excited about the claim that Tsubasa got krokodil from Volgograd somehow. I didn't believe that because I'd not heard of any deaths linked to the drug, but Heinrich was inclined towards sensationalism. One must be if they become furious when you don't acknowledge that algae are protists. *Der Fashionista* Julia advised me to proceed with caution when it came to Tsubasa. Her younger sister had dealt with him and got her liver fucked from something laced with something-or-other. The sister may have bought it from Tsubasa, or someone else; she went to several dealers for different needs. When I pressed Mihai and "MC Eklektik" Andrei about what Julia told me, they assured me that Tsubasa was a safe person to buy from. Immediately afterwards Andrei, at the mention of Julia's sister, went off on graphic tangents about her body.

Mihai gave me Tsubasa's Signal info. We exchanged formalities and set up a time and place for the deal. I made a significant withdrawal from my mother's bank account. When pressed about this, I said that I was getting worried about the validity of our checks. She didn't buy this at all but didn't question me further. She'd known about the *curvă* for years because her friends gossiped like everyone else. She is, however, enough of a pushover that she totally paid for my Helltorso. Everything undesirable to happen to me is her doing.

I was five minutes early for my meeting with Tsubasa in an alley by the Vlad Tepes statue a few streets over from where I lived. Statues of Vlad Tepes are practically an industry in Bucharest, but this one drew me in like none of the others. It was fashioned out of black and green iron, seemingly impervious to rust. Tepes was mounted on a massive horse, which was hilariously more crudely detailed than the Impaler. Like all the statues and busts of him, his face was plastered with the staid ferocity of a bear. He was regally clad and bore his trademark spiked crown; in his outstretched left hand was a long scepter, the handle grooved like a canal system and the head of the scepter was round and squat; great for clobbering and asserting dominance. I couldn't help but impose phallic connotations on that scepter. Occasionally people left trinkets on the base of the statue—decapitated flowers, amateur mixtapes, and lone cigarettes mostly. As I passed the statue over the years, I came to view it as a sort of petty synchronic vending machine. I'd crush the flowers with my sneakers, throw the mixtapes in the waste bin, and smoke the cigarettes to the quick. It became so routine that the Vlad Tepes Vending Machine became an unconscious affair. I never felt like taking a *curvă* and fucking her against the statue because I felt like such an act would disrupt the flow of flowers and cigarettes and mixtapes.

Tsubasa, no older than nineteen, came looking like a quetzal bird: bloody felt hat fit for a pimp; impish, lime-green jacket tapered by black fingerless gloves; dress pants the color of an avocado terminating in motley-colored sneakers. None of this clothing I had seen at local malls. He carried a duffle bag that bore the general anatomy of a Louis-Vuitton but was obviously off-brand, but somehow looked better and more high-dollar.

"I've heard of you, *buddy*." He used the English word, but his accent—a weird clash of Romanian and Japanese—made it sound like *baddie* or *body*.

"Yeah? Who told you about me?"

"Mihai, of course, and others."

"The tattoo, I guess."

"That. And Mihai called you *pasionat*. I like those kinds of people."

I couldn't tell if Tsubasa was being genuine, but the small talk stopped there. Tsubasa pulled four vials of Trenbolone and a baggie full of needles. He pasted a template in the Signal chat—instructions for how to store the vials and inject the Trenbolone. I put the goods in my backpack. Once I paid him, neither me nor Tsubasa spoke or touched each other. I exited the alley discreetly.

My interactions with Tsubasa had been consistently bizarre. He never referred to me as *Alin*, only as *buddy*. During each deal he'd gargle before he'd spit multiple times. I asked Mihai and Andrei about this, and they said that this behavior was unusual for him. I never pressed Tsubasa about his insistence on *buddy*, or where he learned that word. It was the only English word he spoke around me, but Mihai said he was fluent in English. Tsubasa only wore that quetzalesque outfit around me. That was the only outfit anyone saw him in. After a while, it was obvious that he didn't know how to sew clothing.

I bought my mother some *cașcaval* and bread from the usual market, not only to dampen the suspicion that I'd been doing anything illicit but also because there was a genuine need for cheese and bread.

"Thank you, son."

"Mm."

"What else have you been up to?"

"Walking. Just walking."

"It's never just walking."

"To you."

I punched my palm and smiled wickedly. She shrank away. I used the opportunity to go up to my room. It was dark enough to get what sailors called scurvy but light enough to move around uninhibited. I wasn't tidy but my room wasn't outright unbecoming. Books I'd never read littered the floor, posters of bands I'd never listened to or hadn't listened to for years. My bed was perpetually unmade. The blanket looked like the crumpled body of a tuberculosis victim, and often I'd wake up with the mattress cover peeled off the bed and on the floor. I had a mini-fridge full of cheap beer next to my ancient PC where I pissed away time watching videos on dying breeds of masculinity, reading about obscure ethnic groups, and MMOs where I haven't bothered with expansion packs for nearly ten years. I mostly drank Ursus and Silva and the like. My mother never checked the fridge so I could store the vials in there. Storing the needles was more of a challenge. I decided to tuck the baggie beneath the field of socks in my sock drawer.

I had spent too much money that day and didn't feel like hiring a *curvă*. I took out a poster from my collection of Ceauşescu propaganda from under the bed. The poster had been browned but was in otherwise good condition. It depicted Nicolae and Elena side by side against the backdrop of a waving Communist flag. Ceauşescu the Dictator was wearing a gray three-piece with a spotted tie, his orcish face jovial and his Botoxed lips smiling sheepishly. He held a huge bouquet of roses, their crimson heads bright and menstrual. Ceauşescu the Lady was also suited up, hers being cinnabar. Surrounding the Ceauşescus was a herd of young children, in school uniforms and peasant chic alike, groomed to smile for them. I imagined Elena Ceauşescu naked with her ass spread apart, spit in my hand, and masturbated onto the poster. I got some cum on the children, some on Elena, some on Nicolae, some on the Communist flag. I cum with the volume and force of a spitting archerfish. *Curvă* feel it through condoms. I'd use this poster whenever I couldn't find a *curvă* until it got too crumpled to use and I'd have to toss it in the trash, like the others in my collection. It is, admittedly, less of a collection and more of an elaborate, antique tissue box.

This ritual is neither fetishism of nor antagonism against the Ceauşescu regime. It is, instead, an exercise in neutrality. My mother's side were communists. My father's side were hooligans before the war. I am a political Janus. Some of these posters I got from antique stores and eBay sellers. Others I got from my mother. She doesn't know that they have been repossessed and never will.

I hadn't seen a needle since I got the Helltorso done. Injecting the steroids wasn't hard once I had a general grasp of what to do. The injection site hurt for a while. I couldn't get Vlad Tepes and bodybuilders on variety shows out of my mind once I started doping. I was becoming an emperor in plainclothes. The muscles that would develop after a couple of months would be practically and symbolically akin to the colossal antlers of an elk, or the thousand eyes on a peacock's tail.

Andrei turned me on to a bodybuilder friend who came to clubs he performed at to push me further. I hated him, that arrogant dragon Matei, but he served his purpose.

Matei—he had FUCK on his right thigh, YOU on his left thigh, the Leviticus verse about homosexuality on his back, all of it in a disorienting cursive. His voice was bomb-loud, even when we were making small talk. He bragged about family members in the Românească, which confirmed he was lying about it. He told me to shave off my beard when he had a beard himself—a worse one. Matei said he fucked strippers that worked at Maze's. All of them knew his cock, he said. I said to Matei, well, I fuck *curvă*. *Curvă* are nothing, he said; you are pathetic and lonely. He didn't know who he was talking to. At the same time, his life, his body were what I aspired to.

In conjunction with Matei's prescribed workout routine, I altered my diet dramatically, only eating meat and vegetables. Before I started doping, my mother insisted that we eat pork often, as if it was Christmas every week. Yes, come Christmastime I thought the taste of pork was stale. They say the pig dreams of the knife before slaughter, but if the slaughter of pork is premeditated assisted suicide, then the slaughter of fish is murder by a race of gods. So I switched primarily to fish. The best dishes are catfish in garlic and smoked mackerel. I cannot get over the hilarity of vegans quarreling with omnivores over tetrapodal livestock, when the seas are being gutted like the very fish we extract from them. Gods of war sick of sacrifice, so we seek the blood for ourselves.

Three months into my transmutation, Julia finally became interested in me sexually. Julia looked worse naked than she did in her French and Russian designer clothes. She remarked that I was getting acne around my cock the tenth time we fucked.

"Are you going to infect me with something, Alin?"

I replied that she was already infected. She was born in sickness, a breech birth. I shoved two fingers down my throat and gagged to illustrate my point.

"You are sicker than me, Alin. I am afraid of you. People should be afraid of you because you are a sinner."

I told her that sin was a conspiracy of guilt derived from art. That is part of why I got the Helltorso. I want people to be afraid of me because I have been afraid of others my whole life.

Julia spat in my face and left.

Since Julia's comment about my sin, I became obsessed with the number three. *Tres, trois, TREI.* Three canticles in *The Divine Comedy*, three manifestations of God, three panels in *Earthly Delights*. I wanted to cut off my pinky fingers and ring fingers and so I would only have six fingers, a multiple of three. Three primary colors.

Henceforth I only engaged in threesomes. I didn't let marital status deter me; married couples were the best. I'd always make a conscious effort to perform better than the husband. I caused divorces because the boy with the Helltorso was the most ferocious lover in Bucharest. My favorite Protestant is Martin Luther for normalizing the act of divorce.

My threesome binge almost got me killed.

How I loved Iacob! A decade my senior, he worked at a bank and was married to a model that worked for a fetish clothing line based in Timişoara named Elena. Elena's biomass was about a quarter silica, so we found kinship on that front. After three threesomes Elena divorced him. Elena never professed love towards me but after a conversation or two with her, I could see the divorce coming swiftly.

Iacob and I went out for a beer one night. He always wore casual clothing when we were drinking—so casual many would wear his clothes lounging around the house. That night he wore his banker's uniform. We talked for about two hours but the bar, Iacob's favorite, wasn't so cramped or soundproofed enough that we'd have to shout over each other or other people. I comforted him about the divorce as best as I could; he seemingly took it nonchalantly. We walked down a street dominated by highrise-esque hotels and Communist architecture, which made the streetlights dimmer than they were supposed to be. Iacob suddenly turned around and walked the opposite way I was walking. I stood there transfixed and confused.

"*Hei*, Iacob, where are you going?"

Iacob was silent. Iacob stopped in his tracks and turned to face me, some meters away.

"Alin! You know what you did!"

"I don't know what you mean!"

"Elena's gone because of you! She told me!"

"Iacob, that's not my doing!"

"She said she loved a man with Hell on his chest!"

"Elena has said nothing of the sort to me!"

Three hooded and masked men wielding baseball bats emerged from an alley and surrounded Iacob. Hooligan gargoyles. Clearly they were his allies.

"Iacob, who are they!"

"Friends! Friends I have paid!"

"Who pays friends, Iacob!"

The men charged at me. I fled from them, leading them on all sorts of false turns in the labyrinth of Bucharest. A deep hope I had was that, if Iacob and the bat-wielders veered too far off course, they would be murdered by some agitated criminal who happened to be in their path. I managed to escape them after a pursuit that lasted for a couple of hours, without a bone crushed, a patch of skin bruised, or even a brush of air against my person. My heart pounded more than I expected. Some days later, Iacob's body was found, his skull battered by a blunt object—seemingly a baseball bat. The assailant(s) were never caught.

I didn't go to his funeral.

A few nights later I decided to try my hand at seducing men. I hadn't before. I had nothing against men on an aesthetic or sexual level, I was simply too preoccupied with women. I loitered outside the Control Club waiting for some boys to come out. The bass rattled the ground outside and my legs grew numb after a while, so I had to lean on the wall of the club and pace every few minutes. One, hedgehog-haired and looking like a *fabulous* wino, staggered out and fell to the ground. His wallet flew out of his pocket, almost landing in the sewer, and I gave it back to him.

"Thank you."

I helped him up and supported him as we walked.

"Can I fuck you, boy?"

"Uhhh."

"You know, fuck. F-U-C-K."

The boy's speech was slurred like a cauldron of concrete.

"Fuhhh… fuck. Yeah."

"Where do you wanna go?"

"Uhhh… the back."

"Of Control Club?"

"Yeah."

I put him against the wall. We made out for a bit, our breaths and tongues foul. I yanked down his ripped pants and he yelped as I sucked his cock because I had no experience with the organ. The twink was so shitfaced I'm surprised he didn't spray my face with urine. I spat on my own cock and tried to go in his ass, but I went limp. By then, I realized, my cock was actually shrinking. I couldn't get it up again no matter how hard I focused on the shabby twink or on women I found alluring.

"You fuckface! Bring me back here just to go soft!"

The twink punched me in the face. I barely flinched; he was drunk enough and weak enough that it was more of a tap.

"Boy, you don't want to test me!"

I took off my shirt as a display of aggression. As soon as he saw the Helltorso, he backed away. "Oh. You're Alin. I'm sorry. Uhhh…"

The twink stumbled off without another word. I snuck back into the house, put on contemporary Eurobeat and the old brooding Timişoara band Radical din Val for about thirty minutes, grew bored, then slept. I didn't greet my mother in the morning.

That was my first and last sexual experience with a man.

Mihai introduced me to his friend Sadya, a stunning Turkish woman. She worked in porn and Mihai sent me some videos she starred in before we arranged a meeting. The videos were pretentious and overproduced, which made them even more likable. Sadya's hair was raven-black cut with immaculate bangs, her eyes an impenetrable brown. Her face was so evenly formed that looking at it felt obscene. Her lips were always done up infection-red. Sadya's figure, especially naked, was utterly Hellenic: nipples red as cinnamon candies, contours and curves displaying the grace and precision of a ribonucleotide.

The men in those videos fucked her like beasts, like demons. They were inhabitants of the Helltorso. Even though the sex was conventional, watching Sadya get fucked like that felt more lurid than the most bizarre paraphilia. Watching those videos aroused me more than any stimulus my senses had encountered before.

Sadya had been an art student before plunging into the world of pornography, so she took a liking to the Helltorso. Aesthetics were a chief topic of discussion; she knew as much about Turkish epic poetry and arabesques as she did Romanian Symbolism and the Nouveau Roman movement.

Robbe-Grillet, she said to me once in bed, *knew the power of surfaces as intimately as Ottoman architects.*

She was one of those rare people who saw aesthetics in every atom of Creation and, consequently, cast sweeping judgement in aesthetic terms on everything that existed. She said that out of all the men she had been with, I was the most aesthetically pleasing she'd ever encountered.

When Sadya and I decided to seriously date, we rented a luxury apartment near Ferentari. She thought as much as I did that relying on my mother when I was one of the most infamous men in Bucharest was pathetic. It was a respectable abode that we made garish with camp-obscene posters, books in Turkish and French, and a regular botanical garden of cacti. The kitchen constantly reeked of garlic, fish, and cabbage. The bedroom, a lavish space fit for a shah, was ritually desecrated by our sex every morning and night. There were gutted pill bottles littered around the apartment because Sadya had a problem. She said she got hooked back in Ankara, but it came so naturally to her to down pills that it was like taking a dietary supplement.

The American rappers all do it these days, she said. *You know, the ones that sing more than they rap. I feel like an American sometimes.*

Sadya made trap beats herself but hadn't begun selling any on BeatStars or anywhere else yet. Most of the samples came from Turkish folk music. She showed me one, titled "Armed Against Justice" after the Rimbaud line, and within twenty seconds of the beat I knew Sadya would amount to nothing as an artist.

We ate dinner after we fucked one night, and we were talking about the dissolution of the Ceaușescu regime even though it was before our time. It got heated, not because we disagreed on the intrinsic moral or practical value of his policies, but the *aesthetic value* of them. My neutrality was compromised. She left the apartment as soon as I began shouting. Even though this fight was ultimately trite, I was wounded deeply. Sadya reminded me of my mother at that moment.

Even though we made up quickly, I began to work on a project in secret. It was an epic poem designed entirely to spite Sadya. The poem was called *The Progeny of Eve,* and it would be divided into sixty-nine cantos, with each canto divided into six stanzas with nine lines comprising each. The poem would chronicle historical women who I detested (Helen of Troy, Elizabeth Bathory, Catherine the Great…the usual suspects) and blame their failure as humans on the deception of Eve by the Serpent. I gave up after writing thirty-nine stanzas of it. I found it artless. The realization that my magnum opus, my *darling* was without art, little more than an aborted fetus, was the most devastating revelation of my life.

Things became fraught again. We got drunk on Ukrainian chardonnay and we got agitated at each other. It was over Monet.

"Go do your porn," I said, changing the subject.

"I don't want to, Alin. I only want you."

"There are men—men lesser than me yet better than me— that would kill to taste and tenderize your pussy right now."

"I don't care about them. I don't care about Monet right now, either. I only care about you."

"Then quit porn."

"No."

"You're like my mother."

"Your mother! You keep repeating the same horror stories about her. What do you actually have against your mother?"

"She's dumber than Eve."

"What has your mother ever really done to you?"

"She groomed me to be a demon."

"You don't know what grooming is, Alin. I do. From my own mother, even."

"Tell me."

"All I can—and will—tell you is that *you* remind me of *my mother*. My mother was a cunt; a cunt you never paid for, a cunt you couldn't imagine. I bet your mother is a dear old woman who loves you; but of course I wouldn't know, because you keep me all to yourself—do you even talk to Mihai anymore?—so I've never met her. I never had that luxury, and that makes me want to meet your mother even more. You took it for granted. If Satan saw you, he'd throw you back up to Heaven because you're *nothing*."

This went on for hours. We eventually apologized to each other.

Suddenly, she quit porn.

"Why?"

"I don't know. I'm good at what I do. I want to do something else."

"What can you do? Have you done anything else besides porn?"

"I want to be an artist."

"You kept saying porn was your art. Where did that art go, Sadya?"

"I don't know."

"What are we going to do to keep up with the rent?"

"I don't know."

"We'll have to move out!"

"No. I'll find some way."

"I don't trust you in that."

"Why not!"

"You're too used to it. Don't you know where we are? Don't you know Bucharest is a *Sheol* for art? It's not like the old days. The monuments to all those poets and composers don't mean shit. Not even to those who erected them. Art is the new God, Sadya. It is dead, buried in a shallow grave. You're a cultist now. You *deserve oppression* at this point."

"Get your fucking tattoo removed, then! I don't care how long it takes or how much it's gonna cost you!"

"You cannot remove Hell. Even atheists read Dante."

I didn't fuck again Sadya after that. I don't know if she fucked at all after that argument. We stopped sleeping together and switched rooms. For weeks she isolated herself in her room as if she was preparing for hibernation. She did nothing but stare at the ceiling, constantly high, muttering nonsense that she said was songs. I had to sell my remaining cache of dope secondhand to keep the landlord at bay. I didn't care what Tsubasa thought.

One morning, I made my usual coffee and decided to look over *The Progeny of Eve* to see if anything could be salvaged. It was a futile hope from the start, but I was nostalgic for it at times.

The manuscript was gone.

I barged into Sadya's room. The air was stale and frozen. There were depleted bottles strewn across the floor. Pages of manuscript. I didn't have to try and rouse her or feel her pulse. There was no need. Even though Sadya's corpse was before me under her covers, I didn't feel even a fleeting numbness. I called the *poliție* mechanically. When they came to the apartment, they ruled it a suicide immediately. I had not made it to the part in *The Progeny of Eve* where I denigrate Sadya, so I was never considered an accessory to murder. I couldn't have been, anyway. She bought the pills herself.

The autopsy showed that she was pregnant when she died. There was no way it could've been mine. Nobody can understand the existential terror I felt. Another human being was conceived as a direct result of my incompetence. It was an avatar of my failure, an organism that would have mocked me merely by breathing. I had broken-record nightmares in which the child would assume my face and consume me. Patriphagy. To awaken was to be vomited.

The courageous die. Cowards live. I am a coward.

She never mentioned where she got the pills from. I didn't ask or need to. I wondered after she died, however, if she got them from Tsubasa.

I moved back in with my mother out of necessity. My body had sufficiently degenerated from the steroids, and she was shocked by my jaundiced countenance when I walked in the door. The first thing she said to me was that I truly looked like a *strigoi*.

Shortly afterward, I collapsed with searing pain on the stairs. My mother called an *ambulanță* and rushed me to the Royal Hospital. Evidently, I had cysts in my liver, a condition that the doctors called *peliosis hepatis*. I'd need an operation.

I refused surgery against their council.

They said death wouldn't be likely, but if the cysts ruptured, I would bleed internally. For all Romanians talk of the Impaler, they are hilariously frightened of blood—even the idea of blood. The likelihood of death, however, enticed me. For a man with Hell on his chest to go to Hell! Would Sadya be right that Satan would toss me up to God to spite me?

I started composing death poems. Why 'poems' in the plural if there is only one death? I can't be sure how many times I will die, or how often I have died already. I felt fine, but if I could bleed to death at any moment, I wanted a piece of art left behind.

I assured my friends I was fine, and that I would be fine.

Mihai said Tsubasa died. Nobody knew why or how he died, but they found him on the street one day. In all likelihood, Mihai said, he was killed, even though the cause of death wasn't disclosed. When they found Tsubasa, he was face-down and naked.

Poets Die

The papers, dated the third of November, dedicated a negligible block of text to reporting the death of Ezra Pound. The American poet died in his sleep at San Giovanni e Paolo Civil Hospital in Venice as his intestines became clogged faster than any intervention could prevent. His funeral was already held, and he had been interred in the city's municipal cemetery.

Nobody in the nursing home who read the papers, or had the papers read to them by other residents or staff, wept over the news or were aware of Pound's status in American letters or otherwise even passingly. Those who were familiar with Pound—either by reading an isolated piece bearing his authorship in an anthology of verse or merely hearing *Pound* pronounced in full or *P-O-U-N-D* spelled out for confirmation—skimmed the article so that only choice words or key phrases would stick out amid the sporadic blur of ink and paper. The predominant conclusion was that the departure of some mad traitor who hadn't set foot in his own country in many years was of no consequence, to hell with *influence*.

Dom Mulberry read his copy of the November 3rd paper in his wheelchair. He strained his eyes until he felt tired again, then he would compulsively wipe them and his dry, coarse fingers would grow soaked with tears and ocular slime. Dom idly plucked hairs out of his graying, unkempt pencil mustache and rubbed loose strings sprouting from his crumpled, unbuttoned felt vest between his thumbs. His bifocal lenses became streaked with grime. He could concentrate adequately through the din of the other residents, the ventilation system, the garbled coos of the nurses, and the sharp keyclacking and tinny rings emanating from the reception desk; but days after he was admitted to the nursing home, he lost his conception of an *inside voice*.

Dom eventually found the article on the death of Pound deep in the bowels of the day's paper. He was overcome with pity.

"Nurse! I need a pen and paper!"

Dom's voice, even when he shouted, was hoarse and frail. It took Dom several carefully timed attempts over the span of ten minutes to finally acquire his pen and paper.

Dom formed words on the page. They were coherent and eloquent at first, but those words gradually disintegrated into aggravated, infantile scribbles. He threw the aborted page into the crowd in a rage.

A resident Dom didn't know by name or face turned his way briefly as the paper bounced off his right shoulder.

The resident was garbed in a beige sweater mildly stained with drops of brown and yellow sauces, gray trousers noticeably frayed at the cuffs, and black leather loafers that had not been polished for some time. Advanced kyphosis made him bow over, but he did not yet stare at the floor by default. His face was littered with angiomas so prominent that they resembled radish saplings. He wore no spectacles or bifocals, but he squinted at Dom long enough that it would be unreasonable to call his eyesight pristine. The resident's hair, though thinned considerably, grew evenly enough that his hairdo was the sprightliest feature of the man's countenance.

The resident sized Dom up after realizing the paper may have been thrown at him deliberately. Then, wordlessly, the resident resumed reading his own copy of the newspaper. Dom existed as much as Ezra Pound to him.

Fiery pain shot through Dom's hands. He dropped the newspaper and groaned hoarsely. The nurse who gave the writing supplies to Dom—a young woman who, perhaps since birth, didn't appear young at all—marched over to him.

"You're making a scene."

"Pound is dead! *Dead* and *tot* and *dood* and *død*! I can't even write an elegy to him! You don't understand what this means!"

"You're making a scene."

"I'm in pain!"

"You took your medication this morning. I gave it to you. You swallowed it. Washed it down with a glass of water. I didn't have to give it to you again because you didn't spit it back up today."

"It didn't work!"

"Your next dose isn't till tonight."

"I'm in pain!"

"Mr. Mulberry, you know very well that you must follow your medication regimen *exactly*. We should only have to go over this *once*."

"I need something for this goddamn pain! *Something! Some— thi—ing!*"

"Don't exert yourself. You don't want to make the pain worse. I know you don't want that, Mr. Mulberry."

"You pity me—me, and the very grief of the human Spirit itself!"

"Was someone who died here recently your friend?"

"It was Pound! Ezra Pound! I never knew Pound, why should I? The paper says he died in Venice!"

"—We're taking you back to your room, Mr. Mulberry. We can't have you making any more of a scene. You're disturbing the other residents."

Those present to witness this exchange kept to their papers, the walls, the floor and the ceiling. Not one expression in the room shifted a muscle.

"I don't give a goddamn who I'm disturbing! To hell with my room! That is no *room,* but you call it a room out of a promise brimming with nothing! A 'scene'! What does the death of Pound mean compared to a 'scene'? A 'scene' that is a 'scene' in your mind only!"

Dom burnt out his voice as he was escorted to his room. The light was turned off and the nurse kept the room dark. Dom wanted the light back on. The nurse refused to turn it on until Dom's requests shifted to water and food. The nurse scolded him, and when he continued to ask for food and water—then when asking became begging—the nurse struck him across the face until he was mute.

The nurse said before she left the room: "That'll teach you to make a scene."

Dom sat in lingering agony until he finally slept in his chair. The mattress—cleaned as much as the bedding, though so stiff that only deep sleep could make it comfortable—was within arm's reach. When Dom woke up, there was no sunlight in the room, only the gray glow of an overcast sky. He heard no raindrops flicking against the glass, though he could feel a storm coming in an hour's time. The elegy for Ezra Pound that was once in his head was gone. Recalling memories of the diction and structure of the piece was a useless endeavor. Dom couldn't weep despite the porcupine-quilled pain in his heart.

Dom never wanted to know Pound personally. He never wrote to Pound when the poet was interred at St. Elizabeth's, or even when Pound was in good graces in the United States. He left well enough alone even when he had tangential personal connections to Pound. Yet had he written to Pound, he would have never feared his stature in the field of poetry and would be impervious to Pound lampooning his work or the person behind the work. Dom kept idolatry confined to his *idols,* for *idols* should never return favors for devotion.

Dom grew clammy when, some days after the news broke, he tried to recite parts of "Hugh Selwyn Mauberley" once more—one of the few poems he ever wanted to memorize—but he kept mangling the lines and stanzas, as if the ink that gave them shape had turned gangrenous.

Enough of 'Mauberley'—

My body was not ruined by a poem. 'Poem' in the singular, not 'poems' in the plural. A poem in the singular is not worth the sacrifice of a mind still making sense of a body lost.

Birds came to Dom's window: cardinals, swifts, orioles. They came not to comfort Dom but to momentarily invade his space before taking off. They didn't feed, sing, or preen. Only their heads moved. Dom could never make out if there was intent behind the motions of a bird's head beyond dumb reflex. Not once did he ever see a bird blink.

Birds came to his window, but insects and cobwebs did not.

Much of Dom's work, especially his early-to-mid-career output, involved birds but their allure was now gone. Birds—symbols of beauty and gentleness for Dom—were reduced to feathered imps that corrupted the crispness of the air and the majesty of the sky. He believed that both the *to* and the *from* installments of the Canada geese migration were serious omens for meteorological catastrophes and spiritual corruption.

Why haven't I seen a hummingbird in years?

A male ruby-throated hummingbird had darted past his window a few weeks prior to the death of Pound.

He began to hate the breeze which scattered seeds the world over and caressed every leaf in its path sensuously. The leaves were nothing to him anymore. The noises they made, once a fundamental inspiration, agitated him. Dom ceased musing about the world's beauty, began cursing indiscriminately, then grew incapable of forming sentences that didn't contain passionate, elaborate views centered around the dead Tsarist and Edwardian societies and assassination-denial. He acted as though Eisenhower had never contemplated the idea of an interstate highway.

Dom was then beaten more often. He became covered in bruises and his rantings became morbidly loud and animated. At their peak, nobody around Dom recognized that any sound was uttered by anyone or anything, and any suggestion of such was a hallucination.

Eventually, Dom couldn't form sounds at all. He completely lost the use of his hands. He forgot about Pound, then forgot the alphabet itself. Finally, his tear ducts failed him.

Dom's death was never formally announced by the staff to either the residents or Dom's next of kin. The nurses pillaged his room as soon as his corpse left the building. They made a library out of the dumpster.

Y'all are *real ones*:

Maeve—Arturo—Jayaprakash—Ben—Fergus—Damian—
Justin—Quentin—Golnoosh—Clyde—Aaron—Cole—
August—Matthias—Bridget—Gaurav—Sarah—Simon—
Miguel—Brendan—Jude—Iris—Gabriel—Julia—Brody—
Kitty—Cobi—Sailor—Shannon—Quincy—Dorian—
Morgan—Zach—Elise—Zena—Kyle—Marc—Callum—
Hadrian—Josh (x2)—Valerie—Salvattore—and Faye!

☩ C.S. ☩

Colby Smith was born and raised in southern West Virginia and is currently based in Cleveland, Ohio. A member of the Neo-Decadent international art movement, he is the author of *The Ironic Skeletons* (Snuggly Books, 2022) and, with prominent comix artist Josh Bayer, *Fish Turn Colors Then Break In My Hands* (Stone Church Press, 2023). His first poetry collection, *No Moon*, is forthcoming from Outlandish Press.

www.ingramcontent.com/pod-product-compliance
Lightning Source LLC
Chambersburg PA
CBHW031259210726
48287CB00003B/1095